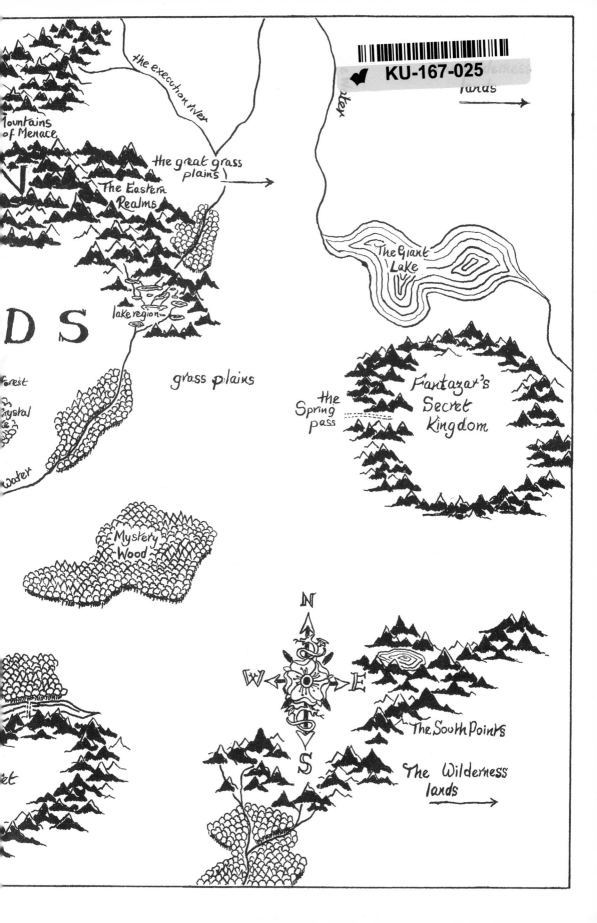

Wrath of the Ice Sorcerer

by

Andrew Bill

Acknowledgements
All characters designed and sculpted by Andrew Bill.
Colour illustrations by John Woodward.
Black and white line illustrations by John Woodward and Andrew Bill.

ISBN 0 9514298 0 9

Author's Note

So many inspired and generous contributions from people in and around Holland Studio Craft have helped with the creation of the book and figurine range, that is Enchantica.

Everyone who has played a part in the genesis of this project, however large or small, has by their interest and shrewd criticisms (whether solicited or not!) shaped and moulded the ever-growing world of Enchantica.

I am reluctant to draw any singular names from the grand melting pot, but feel in a few cases bound to do so:

John Woodward's undying enthusiasm for this project is plainly revealed in his highly imaginative, skilful illustrations. With great patience and dedication he has transformed a series of two and three dimensional designs into the fabulous portrayals you will encounter throughout this tale.

Steven Vyse must be mentioned for his immeasurable help with designing the colour schemes for the Enchantica figurines (and not least for actually dreaming up the name, Enchantica!).

Brian Bill designed the famous Enchantica logo, which now seems so familiar to all of us, and also the highly decorative border on the gift boxes.

I would like to thank Doug Mitchell for his immense contribution and guidance.

Last but by no means least, I give credit to Phillip Holland for his boundless energy and encouragement. For his unwavering faith (which at times was unavoidably blind) which pushed and shoved this endeavour to its eventual conclusion.

There are many more people who fully deserve to be mentioned for their valuable assistance with the development of Enchantica, and I apologise for not naming them personally; but to quote an old cliche — 'they know who they are!'

On a slightly more personal level, I would like to thank certain members of my family and friends; either for their earnest endeavours on my behalf, or their patient sufferance of the turbulent ripples caused by the task of writing this tale . . . . . . and those that will be caused in the future.

A.B.

Do you know Enchantica?
You have been there . . .
In your dreams,
Your nightmares.
Do you know Enchantica?
Close your eyes,
Open your mind,
Escape the chains of disbelief.
Do you know Enchantica?
Then take the hand
of the child within you
And let the adventure begin . . .

Do you know Enchantica?
You are already there.

Contents

Vrorst, the Ice Sorcerer.

The Wrath of
The Ice Sorcerer

Winter crept in with a frosty kiss, framing the leaves and blades with delicate icy beards; and stealthily numbing the lands with the hugging embrace of his frozen voice. The great waterfalls were stilled and made silent, the urgent rivers halted. The northern Green Oaks conceded their final leaves to the violent gales; but stood, snow-kissed and defiant against the biting blizzards that raged through the hills and valleys.

The season of darkness seeped into the plains and woodlands like a slow white disease; painting the landscape the colour of his desire as he came forth from his frozen kingdom.

Drawn upon his magnificent snow chariot, the great Ice Sorcerer smiled at the cruel beauty of the white desert, spreading like a curse over the land at his approach.

He was Vrorst, Lord of Winter, and at his side sat his champion Tuatara, Queen of Witches. With them came Vrorst's minions; Hobgoblins, Ice Trolls, mighty winged serpents, Icedemons, black witches astride fiercesome Snowdragons, army upon army of dark, twisted creatures that marched in endless columns from the frozen north.

Their foul voices rang out in the empty silence; songs and vile chants that taunted the memory of those that ruled the land before them and those that they had indiscriminately slain along their path.

The Citadel of the Wizards lay at the end of their journey, the throne of Enchantica itself.

Vrorst carried with him a crown of ice, specially crafted by the skilled slaves of his frozen palace. They had presented their creation to him in honour of his final succession, for the day when he took his place on the seat of majesty in the high Crystal Chamber; and crowned himself . . .

KING OF THE WORLD!!

Fantazar, Lord of Spring.

Enchantica:
The Legend Unveiled

Try to imagine the world of Enchantica. Before the Grand Betrayal, each of the four seasons was ruled by a wizard of supreme power and majesty; the four Lords of the Brotherhood.

The Sea Star or Enchantica rose, that flourished in the waters flowing around the Forgotten Island, had been adopted by the wizards as the symbol of their unity. Each great lord wore a pendant or brooch in the shape of the beloved flower; and in the centre of the rose there was set a beautifully cut power crystal; to symbolise the colour of his season.

The Forgotten Island was situated in the Southern Ocean. It was barren and deserted; and its shores often shrouded in mist. There was no magic there any more, its soil no longer able to support life; but once it had been a bountiful place.

Legend claimed that the island was where the wizards had first learned of the craft of sorcery and the secrets of life. Some believed that the all powerful 'Spirit in the Mountain', had chosen the four lords and brought them across the sea to Enchantica, to enrich her valleys and plains with the same fruits and flowers, fauna and forests, that they had created in such variety and splendour on their own island.

When they left the island it became a sad and desolate place, the seeds of the flowers fell to earth and remained there, never to germinate. Without the magic of the wizards, nothing would grow.

Each of the four sorcerers had created an orb of crystal. Into this radiant sphere he had sown seeds of magic, nurtured with the food of knowledge. The power of the orbs grew until they became mighty tools of sorcery and the wizards were able to perform the miracle of their seasons wherever they dwelled. The spheres were known as the Fire Orbs; and the great sorcerers were never without them. With the powerful magic of the orbs, the wizards created their Secret Kingdoms in the land of Enchantica.

The first of the four; Fantazar, was made Lord of Spring by his brothers; and claimed a territory in the Eastern corner of the world. Fantazar was unpredictable, riotous and dramatic, his character charged with impatience and vitality. He brought these qualities to his season and exploded it across the world after the slow march of Winter, banishing the white and staining Enchantica green.

The second was Orolan; a strong, forceful being; Loyal, steadfast and radiant. He was chosen as Summer; and he it was who took Fantazar's delicate greens and blazed them across the land, splattering every tree and valley with flourishing foliage; filling every corner with colour and beauty. He shone like the sun in robes of gold and his magic was warm and penetrating like the soothing smile of a long Summer day. He claimed a territory in the South of the world.

Waxifrade was third; a wizard of deep thought and meditation. He was blessed with a wise and generous spirit; and he it was who brought forth the fruits of the land to harvest. He wrinkled the leaves and tugged them gently from the trees. The seeds ripened and dropped before him, holding the precious jewel of new life within them; until the raging of Winter had passed and Spring called them to rise. Waxifrade wore the shades of Autumn leaves; fire and rust, the startling red of sun-kissed berries. His Secret Kingdom was made in the Western corner of the world beneath the splendour of the Autumn sunsets.

Last there was Vrorst; a dark and envious character. Winter was his choice and it seemed to belong with his nature. He was cold and unloving and his magic had always seemed only able to create the seeds of destruction. His brothers knew that of all of them, Vrorst was the most vulnerable to corruption, ambition and malice. After a time, he began to relish the awesome power he had chosen to conduct; the glory of devastation; the stone-cracking power of snow and ice; and the deadly bite of frost. Only in the far reaches of the Northern world could he sustain his frozen kingdom; and he dwelled there, white, like the oceans of snow he sculpted.

After a time, as his brothers feared, the darkness and the cold of his season slowly devoured his soul, turning it to black ice; and soon, the only light that shone from his eyes was the chilling glint of evil.

The four great lords had many followers, faithful servants that proudly wore the colours of their master's season; and dwelled with him, within the Secret Kingdom. The companies of the wizards included; lesser wizards (to tend the Carrier-Dragons), noble witches, fairies, elves, favoured races of men and an assortment of other noble creatures.

The magic of the Fire Orbs spread a blanket of enchantment over the Secret Kingdoms; keeping the land and its inhabitants forever in the embrace of their own season. The world that lay beyond the kingdoms, the Commonlands, enjoyed the passing of all four seasons, each wizard taking his turn to rule over them.

To bring forth their seasons at the appointed time took great power, far more than could be drawn from the Fire Orbs alone. Therefore to achieve the miracle, the four lords had learned how to discover and tap the very life energy of Enchantica itself, an energy that was stored in the form of crystals; four different crystals for the four seasons.

The Spring crystal was Treeflame; a stone which burned with the colours of leafbuds bursting forth with life; and the soft delicate hues of Spring bulbs as they pushed their way through the snow, braving the bite of Winter.

The Summer stone was sunfire; a crystal which seemed to hold within it the piercing rays of its namesake and radiate the warmth and goodness of long Summer days.

The Autumn crystals were known as Bloodstars; to gaze into their scarlet depths was to swim in a dazzling red ocean of dying foliage. The stones mirrored the death of the year, its life blood seeping into its fruits and leaves.

The Three Fairies; Mimmer, Cellandia and Fossfex.

Blackhearts were the gems of Winter; and they were as cold and black as the soul of their master.

The crystals were found deep in the flanks of the largest range of mountains in Enchantica; The Marble Fortress. The Great Spirit of the Mountain also dwelled in the buried halls of the Marble Fortress (in a certain holy peak known simply as 'The Mountain', so it was believed) and it was said that the crystals were the Spirit's gifts of power to the wizards, who ruled in its name.

In the very heart of Enchantica there was a wide lake surrounded by low, forest clad mountains. In the middle of the water there rose an island, connected to the shores of the lake by four long bridges. Built upon the island was a city. An eruption of tightly packed buildings that clung to one another as they climbed ever upwards; towers and ramparts clustered together like the points of a shambling crown; occasionally reaching out to each other with spindly, arched bridges. Beneath them a maze of narrow winding streets and alleys, honeycombed the buildings; and at the points where the four spanning bridges reached the island, massive gates had been erected; emblazoned across each of them was a huge Enchantica rose in solid gold relief.

The city was known as the Throne Citadel and towering at its peak was a lone spire that scraped the very belly of the clouds. At its tip was a chamber encrusted with large circular windows; housed within the Crystal Chamber was the High Throne of Power, the lofty seat from which the four wizards ruled the world.

As the old season drew to its close, the Throne's successor and his entourage would march in glorious triumph and celebration from their Secret Kingdom; and arrive at one of the four long bridges that lay across the lake. They would then parade across the water and hammer on the gates of the Citadel; demanding possession as was their right. The wizard whose power was declining would surrender the seat of authority; and return across the bridge to his Secret Kingdom, to wait once again for the year to turn.

Located in the bowels of the city was the Sacred Chamber, the home of the four chests of power (the Sacred Vessels), in which the crystals were placed. The entrance to this hallowed place was guarded by a High Witch. She alone had the power to open the doors, locked by enchantment, that led through a narrow, dingy tunnel to the bulbous, stone cavern within.

These chests were the very heart of the wizards' power over Enchantica, without them the great lords could never bring their seasons forth on the world.

Once the wizards' season had begun, no more of his crystals would be mined. Those already in his Sacred Vessel would gradually lose their power until they were finally exhausted; and when the next Vessel in line was full, the Throne was vacated for a new wizard; and so it went on.

The power crystals were flown from Dragongorge in the North by Carrier Dragons. The servant beasts would fly with just a handful of precious crystals hanging from their necks in leather pouches; and land at one of the numerous dragonports constructed on the high walls of the city. There to be attended by the lesser wizards, who relieved them of their priceless burdens; and carried the gemstones reverently down to the chamber to place in the chests.

Perhaps it would have been more than sufficient to have a powerful witch and two impassable, magic doors protecting the Sacred Vessels; but the wizards were not satisfied. Using the sorcery of the Fire Orbs, four small Carrier-Dragons were taken into the Sacred Chamber; and transformed into The Guardians.

Fantazar created Gorgoyle, Orolan conjured forth the awesome Arangast, Waxifrade made Snarlgard; and Vrorst transformed a terrified little Carrier-Dragon into Grawlfang, the Terrible. They created four princes amongst dragons, larger and fiercer than any of their kind; and all of them equal in might and majesty. The great beasts were doomed to live their lives buried beneath the citadel, for they had been made too large to return through the narrow tunnel from which they entered; and escape the chamber. For the most part, they lay at the feet of the four marble daises that held the sacred chests; but whenever the magic doors were opened; and the crystal bearers entered the chamber, the dragons reared up, roaring like violent thunder; and belched forth great rivers of flame. Only after the High Witch had calmed them with sweet songs of enchantment, was it possible for the wizards' servants to attend the chests.

With the Sacred Vessels now properly guarded, the wizards could leave the Citadel after their quarterly reigns with their minds at ease, happy to trust the servants of their succeeding brother wizard to care for all four power chests and dragons, as they would their own.

There were many races of Enchanticans that bore no allegiance to any of the wizards; they had their own kings and rulers that governed them and were quite content to live their lives in the changing world of the four seasons. These peoples lived in the regions of Enchantica known as the Commonlands. These comprised any areas of Enchantica not included in the four Secret Kingdoms; and covered the vast majority of the world. Even the Throne Citadel itself fell in the region of the Commonlands.

The inhabitants came in all shapes and sizes, creeds and colours. There were the great cities of Men in the Eastern Hills; five huge settlements crowned with the most magnificent strongholds; each city ruled by a different king; all of them blood relatives to each other. Together they formed one of the most powerful alliances outside the wizards' brotherhood.

Dwelling in the lake regions in the southern foothills of the Eastern Realms were the Raft People. A remarkable race that constructed immense floating cities from rushes woven into great buoyant platforms. One of the strangest and yet most beautiful sights in Enchantica was to gaze on one of the lake cities as it was reflected in the still waters, under the soft blushing light of a deep sunset.

On the northern side of the Eastern Hills were the Mountains of Menace. In places, this range of peaks actually formed the 'walls' of the Ice Sorcerer's frozen kingdom. They were inhabited in the southernmost parts, by the Hobgoblins.

Ruling over this loathsome race was Hellbender, the great goblin king. He had ruled, unchallenged, for more than eighty years, since he had despatched his own

Hellbender, Great Goblin King and Princess Okra.

father, Jemlin, in a battle of supremacy. Hellbender had three children; two sons and a daughter. The sons were twins, Hobba and Bledderag, and their younger sister (regarded by the goblins as a great beauty) was called Okra. The Hobgoblins were hated by both the Eastern men and the Raft People for the evil deeds they perpetrated against their noble neighbours.

In the northernmost peaks of the Mountains of Menace, dwelled another murderous race; the Icedemons. Though not as powerful as the Hobgoblins they were certainly as evil; and possessed the impressive skill of being able to conjure spears of ice out of thin air, a formidable weapon in the thick of battle.

There were many mountainous areas in Enchantica and they were populated by various races of cave dwellers. The most famous of all these were the dwarfs. They lived in one place only; The Marble Fortress. It was the dwarfs who mined the wizards' power crystals. They were a grim but noble race who bore allegiance to no-one but themselves; and chose to make their homes inside the mines; carving their houses out of solid rock. The wizards paid for the labours of the dwarfs in wealth and favours; and it was said that the mountain dwellers had accumulated vast hoards of treasure in the winding tunnels and cavernous chambers of their underground settlements. No-one but the dwarfs knew if such envious rumours were true, for the entrances to the mines were jealously guarded; and only dwarfkind permitted to enter.

The rare and precious power crystals were transported by the dwarfs down from the mines to Dragongorge. The vast, bottomless chasm wrenched its way through the foothills of the Marble Fortress like a snaking dry river. Perched high on its cliffs was Dragonskeep; a huge castle built by the servants of the wizards for the purpose of cleaning and sorting the precious stones. Jutting out from its towers and ramparts like wide open mouths, were the large, hooded dragonports; identical to those found on the Throne Citadel. It was from these lofty platforms that the beasts of burden took to the air for their long journey southwards.

The Carrier-Dragons themselves were cave dwellers. They lived and reared their young in deep cavities in the cliffs. Their piercing cries could be heard echoing up to the surface, as they swooped back and forth, spiralling on the rising thermals; and then diving back down to the craggy depths below.

Other less terrible Commonlanders included the elves and the fairies. They had founded hundreds of small kingdoms the length and breadth of Enchantica, in almost every tree lined valley and wood. They were the only inhabitants of the Commonlands that practised proper magic; they used it to conceal their beautiful kingdoms from unwelcome eyes.

Sweeping down the western side of the Commonlands was the largest forest in Enchantica. The wizards gave it the rather unimaginative name of 'The Great Forest of the West' but those that actually dwelled beneath its thick canopies called it 'The Green Sky'.

Deep in the heart of the Green Sky Forest was the kingdom of the banfs; a secretive race of slightly elfish appearance, more secretive (if such a thing was possible) than the fairies and the elves. The banfs lived so deeply within the forest that it was believed few of them had ever seen the outside world.

The Banf Kingdom consisted of a large city situated at the union of four vast Green Oaks; and a periphery of small villages huddled close to the White Ring. The roots of the four trees writhed and twisted about each other making a labyrinth of caves and tunnels. During the Winter months most of the banfs took shelter in these various nooks and crannies; but for the rest of the year they preferred to live outside in giant fungi called House Mushrooms. Depending on the quality of the soil in which the spores were planted, the mushroom home could develop into a modest cottage or a small mansion. The fungi continued to grow even after numerous rooms had been carved out inside, thus allowing the occupants to add more and more living chambers as the years went by.

The banfs had always lived in close association with the fungi of the forest. They had discovered that all fungi possessed the gift of enchantment; and had learned how to use this secret power; and develop it for their own protection.

Guarding the borders of the kingdom was a wall of tall, white mushrooms known as the White Ring; this fungal, defence barrier emitted a strong force which kept all enemies at bay. Only creatures with a good heart could stand to approach the pure white mushrooms; and pass through to the home of the banfs inside.

The banfs lived in perfect, natural harmony with their gnarled, entwined, thickly overgrown environment. Together with their small dragon-like companions, the terragons; they seemed to live a blissful existence. Only when the evil of the Ice Sorcerer filled the forest with dark bloodthirsty creatures, did they begin to know fear; and be thankful for the shining protection of the magnificent White Ring.

And so the years swept across Enchantica in peaceful succession, each season staining the land its own special colour. The authority of the wizards had its inevitable challengers; but the might of the Brotherhood was never really threatened, they reigned supreme.

However, the Brotherhood itself was not to remain intact. Eventually, the three Wizards of Light lost their faith in the Lord of Winter. His evil ways had grown beyond measure; and he had begun to gather about him creatures of evil and darkness; Hobgoblins, trolls, Icedemons and dark witches were but a few of the loathsome creatures that swore allegiance to the Shadow of Winter. The three lords refused to trust the Throne Citadel; and more importantly the safe keeping of the Sacred Vessels to the servants of Vrorst, so they had no choice but to expel him from the Brotherhood.

The Lord of Winter was forced to construct a great fortress of ice within his frozen kingdom, to house his Sacred Vessel; and its Guardian, Grawlfang (who with the aid of sorcery had been released from the confines of the Sacred Chamber). He was made to relinquish his rights to the Throne Citadel forever; and swore never to march across the Winter bridge again. From that day forward, he directed his season from the frozen kingdom; but it never reached as far south as it had when he sat in the Crystal Chamber. This made him very bitter and hateful

Grawlfang, Guardian of Winter.

and he vowed never to forget what his brothers had done to him; and all his twisted mind could think of was revenge.

In time, Winter became a season of dread for the inhabitants of the Commonlands. Vrorst encouraged his servants to rampage through the woods, valleys, forests and plains, destroying all the good works of the Wizards of Light. When he ruled; and his snows began their slow invasion from the North, a terrible army of dark servants swarmed down with them. Fear and death spread like disease through the lands; and no innocent creature dared to walk out in the open, alone and unprotected, after Autumn had faded. Those days were gone forever.

The five great strongholds of Men gathered their people inside and sealed their doors until Spring; the Enchanted Folk wove their strongest spells to cocoon themselves against the threat of evil; the banfs strengthened the enchantment in the White Ring; and dared not walk beyond it during the dark months.

The three Wizards of Light prayed that the Great Spirit would grow angry at Vrorst's outrages; and remove all the Blackhearts from the mountain stone thus depriving him of power; but to the wizards' dismay the dwarfs continued to mine them; and ship them off by Carrier-Dragon to the North.

It seemed as though the Great Spirit had decided that peace and complacency had reigned for too long in Enchantica; and perhaps the only way to truly rid the world of its evil shadow, was to allow it to grow and gain strength; and in so doing force the hand of good to smite it down, once and forever.

Waxifrade, Lord of Autumn talked with his brothers.

The Betrayal
A hundred years on . . .

In the last few days of Autumn, a messenger arrived by dragonflight from the Ice Sorcerer in the north (heir apparent to the world), the message was that Waxifrade should call a High Council of the wizards to discuss a matter of the greatest importance. Waxifrade was astonished. The conciliatory, almost friendly tone of the message seemed wildly out of character. He wondered what lay behind the Winter wizard's polite request, Vrorst's mind was sure to be boiling with evil intentions; but what could he possibly hope to gain from a meeting of the four wizards?

Using the power of the Fire Orbs, Waxifrade talked with his brothers. They spoke at length of the virtues or folly of such a high meeting; but finally, curiosity overcame their reluctance and a High Council was agreed.

The wizards arrived at the Citadel by dragonsteed, a small entourage of their followers accompanying them. The servants of the wizards were greeted warmly by their Autumn counterparts, although the arrival of Tuatara, the High Witch of Winter and a small party of Hobgoblins and trolls, caused more than a little consternation amongst the noble occupants of the Citadel. The servants of the Ice Sorcerer were placed in quarters as far distant from the rest of the wizards' servants as the Autumnians could manage. They were connected to the main buildings only by a narrow bridge; but as Tuatara quickly noticed, in their haste to isolate Vrorst's servants, the Autumnians had placed them in a darkened corner of the Citadel that could not easily be seen by any of the many watchtowers, a mistake which would later prove to be very costly.

Tuatara, the henchwoman of the Ice Sorcerer, was tall and strikingly elegant. Her skin was deathly pale; and her eyes, piercingly blue and cold, shone forth from her finely carved face like sapphires in the snow. Her long, silky hair was jet black; and when freed from its weaving plaits fell straight and sleek to her waist, the light shimmering down its length like a river in moonlight. She was a woman of strong attraction and charm; but her heart was as black and evil as that of her master; her great beauty belying a cruelty and spite which made even her mightiest enemies afraid. She had come to the Citadel with a purpose; and now she waited for the citizens to quiet before beginning the first stage of Vrorst's grand treachery.

The Ice Sorcerer stood before the assembled council, gathered in the Crystal Chamber at the summit of the High Tower; Waxifrade stared down at him from the High Throne itself, an expression of thinly concealed suspicion on his face.

When the three Wizards of Light had last seen the Ice Sorcerer he had been dressed in the simplest of white robes. Now he was clothed like an Emperor, a dazzling collection of jewels sparkling from his kingly wrappings. His long, sweeping cloak was edged with the finest fur, its luxuriant material studded with extravagant stones, surrounded by the most exquisite embroidery. His power crystal, superbly cut and set in intricate silver filigree, hung by a chain from around a huge circular collar. Unlike the other wizards' crystals, the Blackheart seemed to swallow the light rather than reflect it; and in such a way it truly symbolised Vrorst's evil power; a force that sought to steal all the light from the world and leave in its place, only darkness.

'Won't you tell us why we have been summoned, brother Vrorst?' Orolan Lord of Summer, stood and faced him, he fixed the Ice Sorcerer with a stony gaze, his deep violet eyes, demanding. 'What is this matter of great importance we have to consider?'

Vrorst calmly began to unravel a chart that he held tightly rolled in his hand.

'I have something to show you, brother Summer, if you will allow me.' He slowly rolled out the chart and placed it on a table near to the three wizards. Fantazar rose to his feet to survey the parchment.

'What is the meaning of this Vrorst?' Fantazar demanded.

'Feast your eyes, my brothers,' Vrorst began, 'Behold, the new face of Enchantica'.

At first there was no comment from the three, they simply looked down at the map, trying to decipher the meaning behind the strange drawings. The Throne Citadel was marked. The large, encompassing mass of The Green Sky Forest, which stretched from the mountains in the north-west down to the great river deltas in the south; and the Marble Fortress had also been marked and seemingly unchanged. The Secret Kingdoms of the three Wizards of Light had been drawn with the greatest care and detail; and to the wizards' slight discomfort, were startlingly accurate; but the Secret Kingdom of the Ice Sorcerer was very different. Vrorst had increased his frozen territory by threefold, where once there had been the lakes of the Raft People and the realms of the Eastern Kings; the plains of the heartlands and the fruit forests of the Western foothills, there was now a sweeping blanket of white.

'What does this signify?' Orolan quietly asked.

'My new Kingdom,' Vrorst calmly replied.

'Surely you jest, brother?' Fantazar laughed, 'Have we been called to High Council for some strange entertainment? You cannot be sincere?'

Vrorst said nothing but gave the Spring Wizard his reply with an icy, bloodchilling stare; and Fantazar knew that Vrorst was serious.

'Have you taken leave of your senses, brother Winter?' Fantazar exclaimed.

'These are the lands that you will give me,' Vrorst began, 'To restore the balance!'

'But brother Vrorst,' Waxifrade interrupted, 'How can claiming three times as much Kingdom as the rest of us, restore any balance?'

'Because brother,' Vrorst explained, 'The three of you are in league against me!'

There were shouts of surprise from the other wizards and Orolan made to speak; but his words were drowned as the Ice Sorcerer continued with renewed vigour.

Tuatara, the evil witch.

'For many years now you have plotted together to design my destruction, to deny my right of majesty over Enchantica. You all despise the coming of Winter and the days of darkness; and you loathe my servants who claim the fruits of the land as is their right. Since you banished me to the frozen wastes, each year my reign becomes a little shorter, the days of light a little longer! I have proof that you have corrupted the dwarfs in the mines, persuading them to collect fewer of my crystals, starving me of power.'

'That is untrue!' Fantazar roared.

'The Carrier-Dragons that fly from the gorge to the North are instructed to 'accidentally' jettison a few of my crystals into the wilderness!' Vrorst continued.

'Lies!' Fantazar cried, 'What proof do you have?'

'I have servants that will speak for me,' Vrorst replied.

'Ha!' the Spring Wizard laughed, 'Your servants hardly make reliable witnesses!'

'I consider them reliable!' Vrorst snapped.

'Enough!' Orolan demanded. Vrorst and Fantazar were face to face and seemed almost at the point of striking one another.

Orolan spoke again; 'None of this is new, Vrorst. We have heard all of these accusations a hundred times before. Did you bring us here just so you could continue your insults? Or do you have some positive explanation to make concerning this so-called map of Enchantica?'

'You may not be impressed by my evidence, brother Summer,' Vrorst answered him, 'But rest assured the only important thing is that I believe it. Therefore, in the light of your conspiracy, I demand a kingdom equal to that occupied by all three of your kingdoms!'

'Preposterous!' Waxifrade exclaimed.

Orolan moved towards Vrorst; and began to speak in calm, striking tones.

'Vrorst,' he began, 'Firstly, your accusations are untrue, as well you know. There is no conspiracy against you, there never has been or ever will be. You imagine the traits of jealousy, greed and deceit in your brothers; because you identify them so strongly in yourself and your loathsome servants. We do not covet your lands or your right to reign. The Wizards of Light have always recognised Enchantica's need to her days of darkness. It is a time of rejuvenation, a time when the old year is laid to rest and the new one conceived and born. The reign of Winter is a necessary and vital chapter in the renewal of life. Why should we wish to change this?

It is true that we deplore the murderous deeds of your followers during their months of occupation. The noble inhabitants of Enchantica shrink away in fear when the monsters of Winter take possession of the Commonlands. However, we are willing to tolerate the presence of your servants as a necessary evil, for the sake of peace and harmony.'

'I'm sure that is very kind of you, brother Orolan,' Vrorst sneered, 'But you see, my *loathsome* servants as you rather unkindly call them, are the key to my demands.'

'In what manner are they the key?' Orolan asked.

'If you grant what I ask,' Vrorst began, 'I vow that when Winter spills forth from the frozen gates, only the snow and ice shall lay claim to the Commonlands, my servants will remain with me; safely contained within my new frozen kingdom. It will be as it once was when we four first came to this land, peace and sharing for all!'

'That still does not explain why you need three times as much kingdom as the rest of us!' Fantazar cried.

'It is easily explained, brother,' Vrorst answered him, 'To contain so many fierce and adventurous peoples, I need an area much larger than the one I have. They are not so easily controlled. I would have thought, brothers, that the land I ask for was a small price to pay, for the restoration of order and peace after all these years.'

'Your demands, brother Winter,' Orolan told him, 'Are entirely unreasonable and impossible. They cannot and will not be granted. All four kingdoms were described and laid down in the designing of the world; and they cannot be altered. Even if we had the *power* to grant you your desires; what of the peoples that live in the lands you would lay claim to? The Nomads on the plains, the elves in the valleys and woods, the cities of Men in the hills. Are they to be told to give up their lands, their rights, their heritage, their histories! Simply to satisfy your encompassing greed? The demands that you have brought to this table of High Council are a gross insult to the Old Rules; and you, brother Winter, have shown yourself in your lowest form; a grasping, faithless mountebank, who we were right to cast out. You are still unworthy to share in the honour of the brotherhood!'

Vrorst was unmoved. This reaction to his proposals was exactly as he had wanted; their denial was all part of his plan to divert the wizards' attentions away from what was happening in the rest of the Citadel beneath them. They were angry and disconcerted at his boldness, they were all three intent on beating him down and breaking his spirit; but for all their strong words and denouncement, Vrorst was firmly in control.

'You speak well, my brother,' he said to Orolan, 'But now it is your turn to listen. Perhaps I have not made myself quite clear. It was never my intention to come here this day to debate or argue my demands with the three of you. Rather I came simply to inform you, as a matter of courtesy, of what *will* come to pass. Believe me brothers, I shall take these lands for my own, with or without your consent! But be warned do not try to oppose me or stand against me in any way, for if you do, I shall take it all . . . forever!!'

When he roared the word 'Forever!' his hand came crashing down on the map of Enchantica laid out on the table, his flattened palm completely covering the part of the map where the High Throne of Power had been drawn. The true significance of this gesture was not lost on his brother wizards.

'Your threats, Vrorst,' Orolan raged, 'Might be impressive were they not so empty. It is true that you are entering your ascendancy and that at this moment, even combined, we three do not have the power to stop you. Brother Autumn's Vessel is all but empty, Spring's only half full, mine half of that. Your Vessel, Vrorst, is filled, you have the power to dictate what you will, Enchantica in her entirety is yours for now. However, soon your crystals will begin to fade, your strength will

The Throne Citadel.

fail, and when the first beams of Fantazar's magic shine forth from this tower, all the snows of Winter will be driven back to the gates of your *original* kingdom where they belong, and I promise you, Vrorst, this *will* come to pass. All of your high ambitions, for what they are worth, will prove as temporary as an icicle in the sun!'

'Answer me this, brother Winter,' Fantazar demanded, 'For one quarter of the year you hold the entire world in your hands. Is that not enough? Or has your true intention *always* been to take Enchantica for your own, piece by piece, as your chart suggests?'

Orolan interrupted, 'If this is the truth, Vrorst, you must know that we will never allow it to happen. We shall unite against you and when the power is with us, put an end to your evil intentions.'

'Ha!' Vrorst exclaimed, 'There it is! you deny the existence of a conspiracy but the proof is on your lips, brother! Yes, the power is with me; and I shall take Enchantica as is my right; but my strength will not fail brothers, I will not allow it! If the snows of Winter are *ever* lifted from the face of the world. It will be on my command and mine alone. My threats, brother Summer, are not empty, they are prophecies . . . prophecies of the life to come!'

Vrorst turned and swept out of the chamber. The battle lines had finally been drawn between the forces of light and darkness; and the bitter taste of warfare hung heavily in the air of the wizard's chamber.

'I fear the Ice Sorcerer intends war upon us, brothers,' Orolan spoke sadly.

'Let us unite and destroy him once and forever!' Fantazar urged.

'The world has need for Winter, brother Fantazar; and it cannot be forgotten,' Waxifrade sighed.

'A need for Winter, yes!' Fantazar continued, 'But for 'Vrorst the Usurper', no! Is it not said in certain articles of the Old Rules, that in times of high treason an evil brother may be replaced? Let us consult the ancient scrolls,' he urged, 'To see if they contain a clue to how we may achieve this.'

'To replace the Ice Sorcerer', Orolan spoke, 'First he must be destroyed! There is no other way. Is that not the heaviest of decisions for the three of us to make? Are we so certain that he is deserving of such a fate? It is true that he is guilty of ambitions beyond his right; but please brothers, let us not be too hasty to follow in his footsteps!'

Fantazar turned to Waxifrade for support; but the Autumn Wizard's head was bowed in deep thought, in despair he turned to the large crystal windows and gazed out on to the melting sunset. The red ball of the sun bestowed a shower of starry rubies across the breeze kissed waters of the lake.

'Do we do nothing then?' he said finally. Orolan joined him at the view and placed a firm hand on his shoulder.

'We do as you suggested, my brother. We peruse the ancient scrolls, the residue of the creator's wisdom. Let us re-read the words of the Great Spirit and if we arm ourselves with such knowledge, surely we will win sound victories over he that carries mere mortal weapons.'

As the three wizards consulted the ancient writings, a heavy sadness in their hearts. Vrorst, the Ice Sorcerer, stormed down to the dragon ports to begin his journey back to the frozen wastes, the majority of his entourage following his furious exit. Tuatara did not, she and her small company were busy finishing their evil business down in the bowels of the city, she would join her master at a later date. She still had much evil work to do.

Whilst the four wizards had been locked deep in argument at the High Council, Tuatara and her servants had slipped away from their apartments and stolen down to the secret chambers of the dragons. Their quarters had been so isolated that no-one had seen their clandestine departure, the Autumnians had simply assumed that the Winter creatures were silently entertaining themselves in whichever strange and depraved manner suited their taste.

To reach the Sacred Chamber, Tuatara and her party had to pass through a maze of downward leading dimly lit corridors. To their surprise they discovered that there were no guards stationed at any point along the way; such was the absolute trust the wizards placed in their servants.

The only obstacle between them and the Sacred Chamber was the dwelling place of Quillion, the high witch of Autumn. The corridor that led to the magic doors passed directly through her subterranean home; and there was no evading it. Tuatara decided to approach the house of Quillion alone.

She entered the High Witch's residence and greeted her with a broad smile. She apologised profoundly for disturbing the Autumn Witch; but professed to having an insatiable curiosity of her respected friend and counterpart. The Winter Witch was at her most charming, she enthralled Quillion with her witty chat and broad knowledge, she told the Autumn Witch that sitting in the lonely tower with only her servants for company she had become weary of her intellectual isolation and longed for the stimulating conversation of an equal.

As the goblins and trolls lurked in the shadows of the dim corridor, the two witches laughed and conversed like old friends; with every false, contrived word that flowed like silk from Tuatara's mouth, Quillion became more enamoured with her guest. She began to relax, to enjoy the Ice Witch's company, it was a rare treat for her to have someone to talk to who wasn't a servant or underling. For once Quillion had the chance to enjoy sophisticated conversation; and although she tried valiantly not to forget just who her new friend was, she was determined to make the most of it.

Eventually Tuatara was asked to join the Autumn Witch in a goblet of wine; and although at first she feigned reluctance; secretly, this was the moment the Winter Witch had been waiting for. Hidden behind an ornamental Blackheart stone on her ring was a secret chamber containing powdered Deathhemp root (one of the most potent poisons known in Enchantica). All she needed was an opportunity to slip the draft into Quillion's goblet. Priding herself on being the perfect host Quillion suddenly hurried out of the room to fetch a jar of her special cakes. The moment her back was turned Tuatara poisoned her wine.

The Winter Witch continued her exquisitely charming performance even after Quillion had drained her goblet. Not until the Autumn Witch's eyelids began to drop did Tuatara finish the act and return to her vile self. She wrenched the key

Quillion, The High Witch of Autumn with the Key Talisman.

talisman from Quillion's neck, throwing the dazed witch to the floor, she called to her servants and flew down the short flight of steps to the magic doors that guarded the Sacred Chamber. The Ice Witch slapped the talisman on to the golden dragon emblazoned across the doors; and after what seemed an eternity of waiting, they grudgingly parted before her.

Tuatara had forgotten how unbearably hot it was inside the dark tunnel, the Sacred Chamber itself was just ahead of them, a glowing torch-lit circle at the end of the darkness.

Suddenly, a mighty roar erupted from inside the Chamber, the Guardians had sensed the intruders. Tuatara bade the other creatures remain in the tunnel, an order they were more than delighted to comply with. She moved tentatively forward to peer through the opening; and locate the exact positions of the three dragons.

Just beyond the mouth of the tunnel there was a stone pulpit. This was the vulnerable platform from which the high witches cast their spells of tranquillity over the great beasts. Quillion had stood there that very day when a consignment of Treeflame crystals had arrived for Fantazar's vessel; her soothing voice had calmed the raging dragons; and they had lain down once more to sleep. Beyond the pulpit, arranged in a wide crescent occupying at least half of the rounded floor, were four lavishly carved marble daises, sitting majestically on three of them, were the Sacred Vessels of the Wizards of Light. The fourth dais was empty and thick with layers of ancient dust, its precious occupant long since removed.

The Guardians themselves had been dozing quietly before the dark creatures intrusion, coiled around the marble daises, content and peaceful.

Now they had been roused they were reared up, poised to strike at the first thing that emerged from the tunnel. They waited with bated, fiery breath, anger boiling in their veins like venom, their heads raised high on fully craned necks; and flickering tongues of flame dancing through their teeth with eager anticipation. There would be no time for hesitation, when Tuatara entered the chamber, she would have to stride confidently forward and take to the pulpit in full bewitching voice, if she faltered, the dragons would cremate her.

The goblins and trolls huddled in the darkness behind her, were growing more uncertain of themselves with every moment that passed. The terrible voices of the dragons had effectively dispersed what remnants of courage the creatures had managed to retain after passing through the magic doors and entering the dark, musty tunnel. Among their company, crouched in the darkness, there were three large Ice Trolls; Ogrod, Bogra, and Bolg. Apart from being insurmountably stupid they were also impassable; and quite incapable of turning round in the confined space. Being also seriously lacking in the basic intelligence required to walk backwards; they effectively blocked the tunnel; and as the goblins had unwisely ordered them to bring up the rear, there was no retreat. The only movement open to the goblins and their brethren was forward into the dragons' chamber; but if Tuatara failed to passify the Guardians, that way would mean their deaths.

The creatures watched in mortal fear as the Ice Witch stepped out into the light, there came an even louder cry of outrage from the dragons; and the dark servants braced themselves for the torrent of flame that would surely come blasting into the mouth of the tunnel. Then strange sounds emanated forth from the chamber, beautifully, haunting melodies that skipped from one harsh dragon note to another, soothing their raucous voices and melting their wild menace.

Tuatara remembered her old powers in time. The dragons still recognised her voice after all those years; and responded accordingly. She sang to them in her sweetest tones; a soft lilting spell that sewed invisible threads between the fiercely widened eyelids of the dragons and gently drew them together. The three monsters were slowly eased to the floor by unseen hands, their limbs carefully folded beneath them and their great heads laid softly to rest.

The movements of all three had become dreamlike, their ferocious, ear-splitting roars hushed to long, slumbering breaths. As the last, hypnotic cadence flowed from Tuatara's throat, the dragons slipped into a deep, deep sleep.

The Winter Witch breathed a full sigh of relief. Her magic had worked as well as ever, yet had it failed; had her concentration been stolen for just an instant; the spell would have been broken and the dragons drowned her in fire. Tiny beads of perspiration glistened like pearls across her brow. She smartly wiped them away with a fold of loose material; the array of shiny droplets were not for her subordinates to see and misinterpret.

After stealing a moment's composure, she stepped down from the pulpit and returned to the tunnel. The three large trolls were brought forward. Supervised by the goblins, the lumbering creatures gingerly approached the sleeping dragons, even though the Guardians were clearly quite unconscious the trolls were reluctant to go near. After a few frenzied moments urging and cajoling, they nervously stepped over the coils of the curled bodies to reach for the Sacred Vessels.

Working in pairs, they carefully eased the three precious chests over the rhythmic rise and fall of the dragons' scaly bodies and carried them to the mouth of the tunnel.

The Spring Chest was the heaviest, Tuatara found it to be half full of crystals, the Summer Chest was barely a quarter filled. Her orders were to empty the precious contents into the murky waters of the lake once the grand theft had been completed. The vessels themselves however, were to be spared.

When all three had been removed from their marble homes, the goblins strapped them securely to the trolls' backs and Tuatara led the small raiding party out of the Sacred Chamber to the magic doors. Once again the power of the key amulet was needed, for the doors had closed again behind them after they had entered the tunnel.

The Ice Witch pressed her ear against the crack in the doors to listen for any activity on the other side, it was possible that the body of Quillion had been discovered.

She gripped the talisman around her neck and held it forward. The key kissed the lock and the magic doors sluggishly swung open, the stone steps leading to the High Witch's residence stared back at them. There was no welcoming committee, the Citadel was still blissfully ignorant of their heinous crimes.

The Sacred Vessel of Summer.

Tuatara sent the goblins and the three load bearing trolls stumbling on ahead through the winding corridor leading to the surface, whilst she stole a few precious moments to glance over Quillion's inert form.

The Autumn Witch was sprawled across the floor of her home, the poisoned goblet still gripped tightly in her hand. Strangely, for the first time, Tuatara noticed how beautiful her Autumn sister was; her rich, auburn hair that shone with an almost metallic brilliance, was fanned out over the stone tiles. Her face, although now unnaturally pale, retained a certain serenity unbecoming of the aftermath of such a violent fate. Her lavish robe, fashioned with the most exquisite embroidery in subtly crafted sprays along its length, now lay crumpled around her fallen body.

Tuatara found the full, untouched goblet of wine that had been hers and slowly poured the dark, red liquid over the lifeless body of the Autumn Witch. Quillion's face and hair were splattered in a seeping bloody stain; and the rest of the goblet's contents were emptied in a long, spreading line from the neck to the hem of her pristine robe.

Tuatar's black soul placed a sneering smile on her lips and a cold wicked glint in her eyes, she let the goblet fall on to the tainted body; and hurried into the corridor to follow her servants.

The Ice Witch and the Winter creatures emerged from the last corridor into the darkening twilight of the outside world just after Vrorst and his gathering had flown from the dragonports; following the Ice Sorcerer's dramatic exit from the High Council.

Tuatara and the others were now faced with a problem. How to pass through the open streets; escape through the Winter gates; and cross the great bridge without being seen by the sentries in the watchtowers; and being caught redhanded with their Sacred booty. The Citadel may not have been designed to include guards beneath its surface; but above it, practically every last building, street, or darkened corner was covered by the many pairs of watchful eyes.

The Ice Witch knew that there was simply no chance of a shambling parade of goblins and trolls, struggling through the streets with three large, thinly disguised bundles escaping suspicion. There could only be one answer, she had to create a diversion. Her servants could then slip away through the dark streets in the ensuing confusion; and suddenly she remembered something that would provide her with the means for such a grand distraction.

She ordered her servants to remain in the shadows until they saw her signal, then, covering herself in a magic cloak of darkness, she stole through the streets towards the Winter gates.

Muffled noises of laughter and celebration filtered down from the forest of towers above her as she scurried silently over the cobbles. The Autumnians were entertaining their Spring and Summer guests in joyous style whilst their wizards talked. Snatches of songs and merry poems were lifted into the evening air from the tiny squares of light above; and floated down on the lake breeze to the empty streets below.

Even though the enchanted cloak she wore made her almost invisible in the closing darkness, instinct bade her keep to the shadows and she weaved stealthily from doorway to alleyway, corner to canopy, until she finally reached her destination.

Waiting for her by the huge gates of Winter, casually testing his wings against the brisk breeze, was a Snowdragon. The great white beast had been tethered there on the Ice Sorcerer's command, to ensure that whatever happened with the evil mission at least Tuatara could escape. The fate of the goblins and trolls that had been with her, in the event of failure, would be less fortunate.

The Snowdragon stirred nervously at her approach; but in a moment Tuatara had soothed him enough to allow her to climb into his saddle and take hold of the reins. The Ice Witch turned to look back at the city, now in dark silhouette, its myriad towers soaring before her, piercing the sky. She dared not risk being spotted yet, she needed to create her diversion on the opposite side of the city if it was to be of any use to her servants.

She carefully guided the dragon to the water's edge, making him almost crawl on his belly to avoid being seen. Then they flew low over the surface of the water, the dragon taking only the occasional wingbeat to keep them aloft. The witch steered them as close to the city walls as the dragon could manage, the draught from his wings causing the torches on the Autumn bridge to flutter as he sped over them. As soon as they had rounded the last corner, and the torchlit length of the Summer bridge reached out before them, Tuatara seized the reins firmly and pulled the Snowdragon into a steep climb over the southern stretch of the lake. The Ice Witch urged the dragon higher until the Citadel was far beneath them; a black crown resting on a sheet of shimmering scarlet silk.

The sentry guards in the south towers were just about to settle down for a peaceful night, when an explosion of coloured lights erupted across the sky before them. Exuberant stars and rainbows fell in glittering cascades to the water; the pale walls of the towers and buildings were stained red, green, yellow, and blue, as bolts of bright fire shattered across the firmament. Against the dazzling backdrop, the silhouette of a dragon could be seen; wheeling and diving through the riot of spiralling flares and shooting stars.

Alarm bells rang out in unison across the city; and numerous pairs of confused feet staggered out of doors to investigate the disturbance. Cries of woe were mixed with shouts of joy, as some inhabitants interpreted the streaks of coloured fire dancing in the sky as the first throes of an attack; others seeing them as a surprise entertainment provided by the wizards in honour of the High Council. Whatever the interest, the narrow streets and courtyards were soon bristling with sleepy bodies, all flocking to the southern end of the city to discover the source of the amazing disturbance. In a short while huge crowds had gathered around the Summer gates and along the edge of the water, their heads all tilted upwards towards the heavens. Great streaks of colour twisted across their faces in bright swirling patterns, their eyes wide with childlike wonder.

Suddenly the huge, white dragon swooped down from the centre of a bursting rosette of red fire; screaming low over the crowds, brushing their faces with its swift

Hobba and Bledderag, two evil, black hearts beating as one.

breeze. Then it was away, weaving arrogantly between the tall spikes of the towers; and racing over the glistening spread of the northern waters towards the trees of the lake forest.

The eyes of the watch-towers noticed too late the Winter gates now slightly ajar; and a small, huddled group on the bridge halfway to the shore. Before the distant figures finally disappeared into the curtain of darkness that veiled the mainland, the sentries would swear that in the vague light from the bridge's torches, they saw something being tipped into the yellow-stained waters of the lake.

As Tuatara skimmed the treetops of the Lake forest, perched between the shoulders of the mighty Snowdragon, the goblin raiding party hurried along the dark trails leading through the closely ranked trees to the pre-arranged meeting place; where the dark creatures were to rendezvous with their tribes.

Waiting with the goblin hordes at the forest clearing were Hobba and Bledderag, the twin sons of Hellbender; they had been personaly chosen by the Ice Witch to supervise the concealing of the Sacred Vessels.

Vrorst had decreed that the three chests were to be smuggled into The Green Sky Forest. He would have preferred the chests to be removed much further afield, but time was of the essence; for the three wizards' servants would soon burst forth from the Citadel in pursuit of the robbers.

As soon as the chest-bearers arrived at the clearing, the goblin princes divided the assembled company into one large and three smaller groups. Each vessel-carrying troll was given a small escort of Hobgoblins and Icedemons to guard his progress into the Great Forest of the West. Then they dispersed, each party taking a different route, making certain there was no possibility of all three vessels being retrieved together.

Hobba and Bledderag, who seemed to almost think and move as one creature, remained behind at the meeting place with the main body of the gathering, in order to ambush the armies of pursuers that would soon be pouring forth from the gates of the Citadel.

The crowds of Hobgoblins and Icedemons that followed the twins obeyed the two of them equally, as though they spoke with one voice. They were always together and seemed to share collective thoughts and moods. If Hobba had been angered by a certain individual, the wrath of Bleddrag would also descend on that same unfortunate creature; even if the second twin had not been a witness to the offending incident. The bands of Hobgoblins loved the twins as dearly as they did their father, the great Hellbender; and served them as if they were simply two living halves of the same creature.

The twins were tall, courageous, and charismatic; they inspired the hordes to uncharacteristically brave deeds, encouraging them to fight to the death in battle for the honour of their kind, rather than face the disgrace of defeat. The twins were not at all like the usual breed of hobgoblin, who would always tend towards faint-heartedness when faced with fierce confrontation or self sacrifice. They were insanely valiant, always leading from the front, screaming forth their wild, bloodchilling battle cries as they charged into the fray. The undying courage of the twin princes was only matched by their desperate lust for power and conquest; they were quite prepared to despatch any living being to the netherworld who stood between them and getting what they wanted. This, of course, included their own father (as he himself was only too well aware) with whom they fully intended to fight for the throne of their people one day. Their final plan was to rule in their magnificance together, King Hobba and King Bledderag; two evil, black hearts beating as one.

Tuatara had alighted at the meeting place for a brief moment to assure herself that the goblin princes were in full possession of the Ice Sorcerer's instructions. The chests were most definitely not to be destroyed or damaged in any way. They were to be securely hidden within The Green Sky Forest. Whether by burying, disguising, or concealing, the dark servants were to make certain that all traces of the Sacred Vessels were lost to the three Wizards of Light until it was too late for them to act.

After leaving the company of Hobba and Bledderag, Tuatara continued northwards, her destination was the lofty dwelling places of the mining dwarfs in the Marble Fortress. She was about to perform the second act of Vrorst's grand betrayal.

As the Ice Sorcerer led his flight of dragonsteeds over the frozen borders of his Secret Kingdom, his henchwoman approached the foothills of Mount Cappalla, the first peak of the Marble Fortress.

The Ice Witch had two allies in the dwarf community, Tarbet and Hest. She had met with them secretly on a few clandestine visits, before she and Vrorst had flown to the Throne Citadel for the deceitful High Council with the other wizards. The two dwarfs were not evil, or in any way loyal to the Lord of Winter. Tuatara had simply won them over with her charm and beauty and, of course, her skilfully created lies. The dwarfs led such an insular existence in the remoteness of the mountains, and contact with people from beyond the Marble Fortress was so rare (apart from the small number of dwarfs that journeyed down to Dragonskeep to deliver the crystals to the wizards' servants) that they really had know way of knowing whether the tales that Tuatara told them were true or not.

With her feigned innocence, which she had the power to perform at will, she had told them a catalogue of terrible untruths concerning the Wizards of Light; cleverly using the dwarfs broad ignorance as a weapon to corrupt them.

The two bemused dwarfs could not help but believe the Ice Witch; so conniving were her words. Before she left to fly south with her master, she had urged them to speak with The Circle; the body of government of which both Tarbet and Hest were members, that ruled over the dwarf community.

The dwarfs had never had kings or emperors to govern them, they believed firmly in the virtues of democracy; and the equal sharing of power. Twelve dwarf leaders, who each represented a large number of dwarf families, sat together at a circular table, to lay down the laws and rules which were to shape and govern the lives of their people. Long ago they had decided to use an even number of members at the table, so that no one dwarf would have the power of the casting

Tarbet, Blick, Hepna and Hest labouring in the deep mountain labyrinths.

vote. Consequently some points of law might be argued over and over again for days on end, before stalemate was finally thrashed into conclusion.

For most of the time the dwarfs that served as members of The Circle were just ordinary miners and they laboured quite happily along with their brothers, liberating the power crystals from the deep mountain labyrinths.

Tuatara was predictably met by a mob of suspicious dwarf-guards when she landed at the mines; she was forced to make a hasty explanation at the point of a spear, before eventually being taken to see Tarbet and Hest. The two dwarfs had good news for her. Although the stories she had told them about the Wizards of Light had rocked and subsequently almost divided the whole dwarf community. The Circle, after lengthy deliberation, had decided to allow Tuatara before them, to present her case. The dwarfs told her that she was to feel very honoured by such a dispensation, as never before had an audience with the dwarf government been granted to any outsider; other than the Lords of the Seasons themselves.

Tuatara was delighted, she finally had the chance to use her treacherous talents on the assembled ears of the dwarf leaders; it was what she had been hoping for. Her two innocent pawns, Tarbet and Hest, had effectively sewn the seeds of doubt and fear in the minds of The Circle, it was now up to the Ice Witch to bring the crop to its evil fruition.

On the eve of that same day, a special sitting of The Circle was convened. The stone hall in which the meetings were held, was hidden deep inside the mountains. It was situated at the end of a complicated network of holes and tunnels, the route through which only dwarfs had knowledge. Tuatara was blindfolded to be led through; the dwarfs explained to her that this was a necessary precaution because she would have to be taken past the entrances to some of the crystal mines themselves; the exact location of which had always been kept highly secret.

Eventually she arrived at the Hall of The Circle. The chamber was dominated by an ornately carved stone ring, twelve rudimentary seats had been hewn out of the same slab of rock and were positioned equally around its circumference. The table had a narrow gap that allowed the speaker to stand in the inner circle to argue their cases. Tuatara was left inside this enclosed area to await the arrival of the twelve dwarf leaders. The walls of the chamber were smooth and flat, only the most conservative of carvings decorating their plain faces. The dwarfs were obviously a people who had little time for effort-wasting ostentation and frivolous ornament, they would clearly have rather spent their hours on more profitable occupation in the mines.

Finally, the twelve dwarf leaders filed into the hall and Tuatara's blindfold was removed. Their faces were set in solemn concentration, the only sound they made was the resounding hollow clip-clop of their armoured boots as they trod the stone floor; in continued silence they each took their places round the table.

Tarbet quickly rose to his feet again and presented the Ice Witch to the assembly; after a chorus of private mutterings, Tuatara was invited to speak.

She allowed an atmosphere of tense anticipation to build before she finally began. She spoke earnestly and emotionally, meticulously picking out all twelve pairs of eyes with her own and burning the power of her lies into their minds; twisting and moulding their disbelief like a piece of clay, until she could manipulate their every whim and thought to her own design.

'You my gracious Dwarflords, have been the innocent dupes of the Wizards of Light for far too long,' she told them, 'Or the Wizards of Hate as we now call them. You must not allow them to destroy you as they have my lord.'

Hest rose swiftly to his feet.

'The Lord Vrorst is dead?' he cried.

'No my Lord,' Tuatara turned to him, 'He is not dead; but he *is* broken. The so-called noble wizards invited my good lord to a High Council at the Throne Citadel. He went in good faith, I accompanied him with a small party of followers. The Good Lord Vrorst and myself are the only two to escape with our lives. She feigned a slight emotional attack. Hest gently encouraged her with his kindly tones.

'Won't you tell us what happened, my Lady?' he said, 'In your own time.' 'The wizards called it a council of peace and reconciliation,' Tuatara began. 'They claimed that they wished to invite Lord Vrorst to rejoin The Brotherhood, something he has longed for with all his heart for many, many years . . . but it was a foul trap. In truth, they meant to kill him!'

'But why, Lady Tuatara!' A dwarf called Hepna asked. 'Why would the three wizards do such a terrible thing?' There was a look of pain and confusion in his eyes, he was clearly, deeply distressed at the disturbing events that the Ice Witch described.

'To whom do I have the honour of speaking, my Lord?' Tuatara asked him. He blushed a little as he spoke his name and then with a few embarrassed glances at his fellows retook his seat. Tuatara continued in her clever, dramatic fashion.

'Well then my dear Hepna,' she said, 'I shall tell you why. I shall tell you why the Good Lord Vrorst was coaxed to the Throne of Power under false pretences and then cast in chains and tortured like a criminal. Why, my gracious Dwarflords? Because the Wizards of Light are consumed with loathsome greed and jealousy! For centuries they have coveted the wealth and magnificence of the kingdom of ice. Destroying the Lord Vrorst would allow them to take possession of the north kingdom and all its inhabitants. We, the humble servants of our good lord would become the wizards' slaves. They hate the Winter for its strength and beauty; the fragile perfection of a snowflake, the exquisite delicacy of frost-fringed crispen leaves.

My lords of dwarfs, I come before you as the desperate voice of a deeply wounded lord, the Wizards of Light will stop at nothing to pursue their dark ambitions. Even your homes here are under threat. I must tell you that the wizards have plans to replace your people with their own servants, so that they alone control the source of their power. Is that not an act of naked aggression against the free peoples of Enchantica?

You alone have the power to cease their madness, to silence their evil. The future and the fate of our whole world . . . lies in your hands!'

24

She paused for a profound moment and pretended to choke on a sob, she cast a few enigmatic dewy glances at each of the twelve dwarfs. A tear obediently trickled down her cheek and she made a large show of wiping it away.

'I have nothing more to say . . .' Her words decayed into a rush of well executed, lip-quivering sobs, her soul-wrenching eyes mercifully fell to the floor as if to spare the members the full brunt of her desperate grief.

She expected a clamour of excited voices to reverberate around the walls of stone; a dozen angry, questioning shouts demanding explanation or proof; but nothing happened. Silence thundered around the hall, the faces of the twelve dwarfs were set in grim contemplation, no-one moved, no-one spoke. Their eyes stared aimlessly ahead, each dwarf seemingly wrestling with his own furious thoughts in some far away, blank void. The effect was quite disconcerting and Tuatara suddenly felt a little afraid; were they hypnotized? Had she been careless with her powers and brought magic into her performance, casting an involuntary bewitchment over her audience?

She had been warned by the Ice Sorcerer not to interfere with the free-will of the dwarfs; their independence was the key to Vrorst's success. They were to be convinced by means of argument and persuasion, not the strong arm of sorcery. After all, the Wizards of Light had magical powers also, and spells could easily be broken and replaced by other spells; but free-will was like a rock, firm and steadfast. It could withstand the raging storms of magic, the battering seas of enchantment, the knifing winds of sorcery, and then be rediscovered just as it was before, unstirred and unchanged.

The Ice Sorcerer knew that once the dwarfs had pledged their support to him, nothing in the world would move them; they would turn their backs on The Brotherhood; and work only for the cause of Winter.

Tuatara felt like screaming as the panic rose within her. What had she done? What was wrong with them? The Dwarflords sat around her motionless, as if they had finally become one with their environment, there was no sound except the cold breathing silnce of the stone chamber.

Hepna the dwarf was floundering in a maelstrom of deep thought. There were a hundred questions he wanted to ask the Lady Tuatara.

What proof did she have? Why had the noble wizards suddenly changed so drastically? Why would they treat their brother wizard in such a cruel fashion? How did she and the Ice Sorcerer escape from the Citadel? Why had no-one from the other side attempted to speak to The Circle? Why did the dwarf community have to be involved in the complicated power struggles of the wizards?

Like the other dwarfs he didn't attempt to voice any of these important questions because at the back of his mind something told him the Ice Witch would have a perfectly logical explanation prepared for anything he and the others might care to ask. As Tarbet and Hest had done before him, he had become blinded by the Ice Witch's enchanting persona; he was convinced she was telling the truth. It seemed almost criminal to think the opposite of such a fine, gracious lady.

'Dwarfs!' one of them finally spoke forth, causing Tuatara to almost evacuate her skin. The speaker was Blick and in the time-honoured fashion he rose to his feet to address his brothers.

'Dwarfs, we have to vote, as is our custom. Do we deny the Wizards of Light their source of power as the Lady Tuatara requests, or do we continue as before? Those in favour of denial!'

Twelve voices rang out as one.

'Aye!'

'Against?'

There were no votes left, the motion had been carried unanimously.

'May I propose brothers, that we give the Wizards of Light thirty days to answer the accusations against them. If no word reaches us by that time, we act according to our convictions and seal the mines that fuel the corrupted powers of the three wizards. How do you speak?'

'Aye!' A second unanimous vote.

'Against?'

And so Tuatara's work was done. She had championed her master's schemes with breathtaking success, the final act of Vrorst's grand betrayal had been expertly laid into place; the victory was unquestionably his.

The Ice Witch flew from the Marble Fortress on her swift, white dragonsteed and turned northwards to rejoin her Ice Lord. They were reunited at the gates of his kingdom, she climbed up beside him on his mighty snow chariot that was standing at the head of an immense, terrible army. At their feet wrapped in the purest white furs was the freshly filled Vessel of Winter; and drawing the luxuriant chariot was the great Grawlfang in all his awesome malevolence. The long procession started and the slow journey into the Commonlands began. For the first time in a hundred years the Lord of Winter was marching to take possession of the Throne of Power. A new Winter's dawn was rising over Enchantica and the world would endure many dark days before the delicate green spears of Spring stabbed through the endless snow and heralded the sun.

The three Wizards of Light knew of their loss and were in deep sorrow. Quillion had been discovered in her desecrated state on the floor of her home. At first the wizards had thought the wine to be blood and that Quillion had been the victim of a frenzied stabbing. They soon learned this not to be true, for despite the evil potency of Tuatara's poison, by some miracle, Quillion was found to be alive. Perhaps it had been the power of her own sorcery that had saved her, no-one could be certain; but after a few days convalescence she felt strong enough to carry out the few duties Tuatara had left her to perform.

The Guardians had been discovered deep in enchanted slumber when the wizards entered the Sacred Chamber. The Ice Witch had kept possession of the key talisman in order to hinder the wizards' pursuit of the robbers; and the three Lords had been forced to wrench the magic doors asunder with the force of the Fire Orbs.

They swiftly broke the spell on the dragons and raised them from their dreams; the great beasts roared in violent grief and despair when they realised their loss; and suddenly a light of hellish anger sprang into their eyes.

The wizards calmed them once more and the beasts laid down their heads in quiet submission. The three Lords decided that a mass issue from the Citadel in pursuit of the chests would prove ultimately fruitless, it would also be exactly what the Ice Sorcerer was expecting; and they had played the game on his terms for the last time. The Lords of Light had devised a more subtle plan, a much surer way of retrieving the Sacred Vessels; and so they laid their palms on the dragons' brows and began to chant soft verses. In their other hands they held the Fire Orbs aloft; and as they spoke, strange lights began to glow and dance inside.

Suddenly the whole chamber was filled with dazzling stars and comets, a kaleidoscope of nameless shapes and forms that swirled across the walls, spinning and racing through the air. As the wizards' voices climbed and quickened, so the colours became more vivid and frantic. Their faces were stained with a moving mosaic of sparkling hues; eventually, the activity within the chamber surged towards a frenzied climax, the painted walls almost burning with light. At its crescendo, a volley of shooting stars erupted from the Fire Orbs, soaring upwards and exploding across the stone ceiling; then they showered down again in twisting curtains of gold and silver rain.

Gradually all the lights returned to the Orbs, their glow slowly dying until the crystal spheres were empty once more. The enchantment completed, the wizards lifted their hands from the dragons' heads, the three Guardians calmly rose to their feet and turned their heads upwards to the ceiling of the chamber. A large patch of open sky gazed down at them, stars blinked like distant jewels set in the darkest velvet; the roof of the Sacred Chamber was gone.

Orolan, Lord of Summer, spoke to the dragons.

'The door of the world is now open to you, mightiest of dragons, you know what you must do?'

The dragons nodded solemnly.

'Have we not just given you the power of speech?' Orolan cried. 'Answer me!'

The dragons croaked and stuttered as they tried to work their tongues around their new gift, eventually Arangast, Guardian of Summer voiced his first comprehensible string of words.

'We hear you Lord,' he said.

'We hear you,' the others followed.

Orolan smiled back at them.

'That is good,' he said, 'We have also bestowed on you, by the power of The Fire Orbs, the gift of knowledge. Knowledge of the world you have never seen. You will need to know of the places where your quest might take you, of the people who inhabit the Commonlands, who may wish to aid or betray you. The servants of the Ice Sorcerer have violated the sanctity of this hallowed place; and removed the Sacred Vessels for the purpose of evil. The Winter Servants are our enemies and they must not be allowed to prosper in their vile enterprise.

Wherever they have taken the Vessels, you must follow, if they lead you to the far edges of the world, you must pursue them; and if days should turn to months, and months to years, you must not rest until you find them. For the sake of the world and all its children, you *have* to find them!' Orolan raised his eyes to the stars, held his arms aloft, and with a thunderous voice he cried;

'Go! Go, my faithful ones! Fly! For the sake of the world! Fly!'

Suddenly there was a great thrashing of wings and for a few furious moments the wizards' hair and beards were swept back by a great rush of wind as the dragons scrambled through the air towards the open roof of the chamber.

Clusters of stars were put out as the great shadows struggled through the breach in the roof and emerged into the night sky. Then the three sad lords were alone, in the ruins of their Sacred Chamber; they stared through the gaping hole long after the last dragon had mingled with the darkness; and disappeared from sight. They were now truly alone. Their instruments of power were gone, they could no longer serve Enchantica as lords of the seasons; their authority had been denied them; they were powerless. Soon the bad tidings from the Marble Fortress would reach them; and they would learn of the corrupting of the dwarfs. There would be no hope of reaching the mines before the deadline, so the wizards would decide to withdraw their servants from Drangonskeep and gather all their followers about them for a grand retreat.

There was no alternative but to flee. The wizards would certainly not give Vrorst the satisfaction of claiming them as his prisoners, so together they decided to remove themselves from his reach by returning to the relative safety of the Forgotten Island. They would defend themselves from Vrorst's advance by combining the power of the three Fire Orbs, and with their servants wait in the vain hope that the Guardians would find the Sacred Vessels and somehow return them to their rightful possessors.

The wizards felt ashamed for abandoning the noble peoples of the world to the mercy of the Ice Sorcerer and his murderous hordes, but choice, like power, had been denied them. They were impotent against the force of the Winter Vessel; and their only chance of survival was to escape to the island and bide their time until the tides of fortune once again turned in their favour . . .

. . . and so followed the wrath of the Ice Sorcerer!

A Narrow Escape

Far beneath the towering roof of the The Green Sky Forest, a young banf and his terragon were just waking from a comfortable night's sleep amongst the soft ferns and mosses, nestled under the eaves of a spreading House Mushroom.

Jonquil the banf, slowly opened his eyes and focused on the underside of the huge mushroom, its gills fanning outwards above him like the pages of a giant book. Beyond the thin, ragged curtain of skin that hung down from its rim, the drifting morning mist transformed the twisted trees into pale stains on a floating grey backcloth.

Jonquil and his companion, Rattajack, lay entwined around each other, the banf using the terragon's soft, scaly body as a pillow and Rattajack resting his chin lightly on Jonquil's lap.

The terragon tentatively sniffed the air, it smelled cold and not for the first time during their long journey, he wished he was snuggled up in his warm, cosy nest back in the Banf Kingdom. Although he hadn't ventured to open his eyes yet, with his special senses, he knew Jonquil was awake. The terragon reluctantly peeled them open and blinked drowsily at the dimly lit world about him, it looked even more damp and dismal than the morning before, the Autumn seemed to be retreating faster than ever this year.

Suddenly Jonquil was gone from his side and up on his feet looking down at him, a mocking smile playing across his lips.

'Come on, sleepy head,' he teased, 'How much more beauty sleep do you want?'

The terragon turned his head slightly and fixed the banf with a sparkling, bright-amber eye, the arrow at the end of his tail slipped secretly under a pile of crusty leaves, waiting for the right moment .

'It's a good job one of us can make a move in the mornings, otherwise we would by lying there all day!' Jonquil continued, he bent lower to peer at the terragon, an expression of comic sleepiness on his face. With a sly flick of Rattajack's tail the pile of dead leaves flew into the air, showering the banf's head and shoulders, with a cloud of brown debris, in a fit of surprised laughter and curses the banf staggered back to brush himself clean.

'Just you wait!' he cried, spitting out a mouthful of dried leaves and trying to remove a small twig from one of his pig-tails.

'I'll get you when you're not looking and rub your terragon nose in it!'

Rattajack piped in defiance at him and snapped playfully at Jonquil's ankles, the banf dodged his friendly attack and seized the vine ball from beneath the House Mushroom, he bounced it gently on the terragon's snout and then hurled it through the trees. He watched it land in the middle of a growth of Honey Fungus, the small green dragon scampering after it in hot pursuit. The terragon eventually caught up with his prized possession and dived into the bed of yellow mushrooms, Jonquil called to him, telling him to bring the ball back; but for a few moments Rattajack just lay there smiling at him, as if to say, 'Nah! This is my ball!'

It had taken Jonquil the best part of a whole day to weave endless lengths of treevines together to make the terragon's plaything; but it had been worth it just to see his companion's face light up when he presented the ball to him. Their long, arduous journey had certainly been made a lot more enjoyable by the numerous games the two of them had invented whilst they had kicked and thrown the ball through the forest trees.

When Rattajack finally trotted back to the House Mushroom, Jonquil was carefully breaking up the remainder of the Fallen Star that they had found two days before. The rare mushroom, easily the most delicious of its kind had already provided them with many sumptuous meals, (for the wonderful thing about Fallen Star was that no matter how much you consumed, you never tired of it. The more you ate, the more delicious it became). Remarkably, they had discovered two large specimens during their return from this last expedition, a very lucky find, which was in no small way due to Rattajack's keen sense of smell.

An unwelcome shiver wriggled its way along Rattajack's spine only shaking itself free at his shoulders, he didn't usually feel the cold but the bedding he had slept on had been damp. It seemed that even beneath the gently enchanted shelter of the House Mushroom, where the ferns and mosses were always softest and most inviting, the cold fingers of Winter had begun to take grasp.

The terragon turned to Jonquil, the banf had finished preparing breakfast and was now staring mournfully at a handful of dead leaves, tiny stars of light danced across his palm. He tipped his hand and the small collection fluttered to the ground in lazy spirals. Beyond the protecting rim of the mushroom, the whole of the forest carpet had been showered with sparkling diamonds, it was frost; the first kiss of Winter.

Jonquil the Wanderer, was a strong, energetic, young banf with a taste for adventure. Endless walking and climbing had made him tough and sinewy, his fellows considered he showed a touch more bone-structure in his face than was quite comfortable. He had pale, softly carved features with piercing green eyes that stared out from beneath a curled lock of rich, chestnut hair. The rest of his hair was tied up into three pigtails, in the time-honoured fashion of the banfs, the last of which snaked down into the hood of his shoulder-cloak. His ears were long and pointed and seemed over-large in comparison to his head; but in a twilight world where danger only betrayed itself by the snapping of twigs or the rustling of leaves, the gift of good hearing was invaluable.

Rattajack, his lifelong companion, shared this feature of large ears, as did many other creatures that inhabited the dense forest, he also possessed a superb sense of smell, which on many occasions had proved to be a vital asset. He was pale green in colour with a fiery orange underbelly, his eyes were two gleaming, amber orbs set in a noble, slightly comical face and his long slender head ended in a blunt, rounded snout. He looked every bit as harmless as he truly was, although like his

Rattajack, Jonquil's lifelong companion.

fellow terragons he was guilty of occasionally letting rip with a pleasantly wicked sense of humour.

He could fly, if only for short distances, a characteristic he shared with the dragons, with whom he was very distantly related; but for the most part he chose to remain on foot, saving his power of flight only for emergencies.

Jonquil and Rattajack sat down to a veritable banquet as they breakfasted on the remains of the Fallen Star, it was to be their last meal before they completed their journey and returned to the Banf Kingdom.

This latest adventure had been something of a disappointment, they had followed the narrow, winding forest trails for days on end and not discovered a single troll. One might consider that a good thing; but the two companions *wanted* to find some of the lumbering creatures, they had a game, a rather dangerous game, that they liked to play; it was called "troll-baiting". It involved setting out at night, the only time the trolls were active, finding one of the slow witted creatures and taunting it by throwing stones and sticks. When the quick tempered beasts were sufficiently annoyed, they gave chase, cursing the banf and the terragon, vowing injury and murder when they got their hands on them. The two companions were always careful to stay one step ahead of their furious pursuers, leading them in wild, confusing circles, ducking the large branches that were hurled at them or diving into thick undergrowth only to emerge again in a totally different place. Eventually, the exhausted trolls would stagger to a halt and reach out to rest themselves against the nearest tree, their fat, ugly faces pressed hard to the bark, sweat pouring in glistening rivulets from their foreheads and their heavy chests pounding with the effort of the chase. The object of the game was to keep the trolls tramping endlessly around the forest on a wild banf-chase until the break of day; and then sit back and watch the hilarious spectacle as one of the dim creatures realised it had been caught out by the dawn and thundered through the undergrowth, desperately trying to remember the way back to its hole or cave.

Of course, Jonquil and Rattajack only played this game with the Common Trolls, resident fiends! of the forest, by the time the large, extremely dangerous, Ice Trolls arrived in The Green Sky, the two companions were safely returned to the banf kingdom, under the protection of the powerful White Ring.

The banf and the terragon finished their breakfast and set off towards home along the shady, enclosed forest trail, they were less than half a day's walk from The White Ring.

When they had set out from the Banf Kingdom a few days before, only a handful of fallen leaves had skipped and chased about their feet in the petulant breezes, in the short time they had been away it seemed the very roof of the forest had tumbled to the ground. Autumn was accelerating towards Winter at a frightening rate, Jonquil could feel the breath of the Ice Tyrant and knew that he was poised, like a great menace, to lay his mark upon their land.

As they thrashed their way knee-deep through the swamp of frosty leaves, the banf grew a little concerned about the amount of noise the two of them were making, he was afraid to think how many hostile ears may have been listening.

The forest was full of danger, not only from the trolls, there were other large enemies, only too willing to indulge in a meal of fresh banf or terragon. Amongst these was The Swamp Demon, an infamous monster that specialised in hunting those inhabitants of the Banf Kingdom that dared to venture beyond The White Ring. Tales of its murderous exploits dominated the fireside stories of old banfs as they recalled the tragic loss of brothers or friends, although strangely, only one living banf claimed to have actually laid eyes on the evil beast; and he was Old Yargle.

Jonquil had heard the tale of Old Yargle and The Swamp Demon many times over; as youngsters, he and his friends had plagued the old banf to tell them the story over and over again. There they would sit, huddled together, faces aglow in the light from the dying embers, enjoying every minute of it as Old Yargle repeatedly scared them out of their wits. As he grew up, however, Jonquil began to believe in the story less and less. Over the years the famous tale seemed to have slipped into the realms of fairy stories and fables. The Swamp Demon had become a mythical monster that only really existed in the misty depths of the old one's memory and the excitable nightmares of imaginative banf children.

Jonquil was soon to learn how wrong he was.

They had been battling through the leaves for quite some time and their legs were beginning to ache, occasionally there were places where the sharp forest draughts had cleared the leaf-piles away and they could walk on the exposed ground. These brief respites, although relished when they occurred, did little to improve their progress through the forest, which had become painfully slow. Despite the fact that Jonquil was beginning to doubt whether they would make The White Ring before dark, they had to rest, if only for Rattajack's sake. The banf could have trudged on for some time yet but the terragon was struggling along half buried in leaves, he must have forgotten what his short legs looked like, he was almost swimming.

The only really safe place for them to rest was under a House Mushroom or some other suitable fungi, trolls were fearful of mushrooms and never interfered with them. Of course, it was daytime now and all the Common Trolls would be sleeping but as they were drawing so close to Winter, they dared not take any chances; Ice Trolls hunted by day and night.

They had seen quite a few decent sized House Mushrooms along the trail since they had left camp early that morning but they had passed the last one a good while ago. The mushrooms always grew close to the gnarled roots of ancient Green Oaks, unfortunately they now seemed to be in a part of the forest populated mainly by Iron Beech and Silver Plane trees, the Green Oaks were few and far between.

The two companions were just rounding a rather large, intrusive evergreen bush that had decided to indulge in eruptive growth right in the middle of the forest trail, when Jonquil saw something in the near distance that made his heart gladden.

A little way off the track there was a modest clearing and standing proudly at its far edge was a beautiful towering Green Oak, with three House Mushrooms of more than generous proportions flourishing beneath its enormous canopy.

Old Yargle and Chuckwalla, fireside tales.

Jonquil reached down and gave the terragon a friendly hug.

'Now that's what I call a sight for sore eyes, eh Ratters?'

Rattajack managed to return a weary nod and the two of them were just about to plough on, through the leafy depths towards the small clearing when suddenly, the terragon spun around, kicking clouds of dry leaves into the air and almost knocking Jonquil's feet from under him with his tail. For the second time that day the banf found himself removing pieces of forest litter from his mouth and hair, at first he thought this was just another one of Rattajack's surprise jokes but when he turned to reprimand him he noticed the terragon was staring rigidly back down the forest trail, ears pulled forward, eyes blazing, his nose twitching frantically.

Jonquil knew better than to dismiss this as mere jesting, Rattajack's finely tuned senses had been alerted by a movement in the forest behind them. Jonquil tilted his head slightly and strained to catch any sound, he could hear nothing. Either side of the forest trail, the ground bristled with thorny bushes and briars, there were thick coverings of low spreading shrubs and banks of tall, seeding herbs, sufficient hiding places to conceal an army of banfs but there were no thickets or bushy growths substantial enough to shield a pursuing troll. Even so, Jonquil was in no mind to take risks, he reached down and plucked out two or three of the special Fallon leaves that hung in layers from his lower leg and quickly threaded them through the tight weave of Rattajack's treevine collar, then he dragged the terragon away from the trail and the two of them marched nervously towards the tree.

The creature watched them set off, pushing their way through the tangle of stems and branches that bordered the forest trail. It had cleverly flattened itself against the forest floor, changing the colour of its warty skin to a mottled pattern of browns, reds and golds, that enabled it to melt effortlessly into the sun dappled leaves. When the two companions finally overcame their suspicions and made a move towards the Green Oak, the creature picked itself up, turned a shade of green and crept behind a thickly grown screen of writhing treevines, with which it now blended perfectly. It was a patient creature and would wait for the right moment to strike, it had hunted these slippery banf-things before and although they were often troublesome to catch, they were well worth the hunt.

Jonquil and Rattajack were striding across the clearing with long, ground-eating steps, only a thin line between the two of them and total panic, they both had the uneasy feeling that hostile eyes were upon them. Rattajack started to whimper, his large, sensitive ears couldn't decide whether to listen ahead, behind or to the sides, his eyes were almost bursting from their sockets with fearful apprehension. His tension was spreading rapidly to Jonquil, the banf had to keep forcing himself to stare ahead and concentrate on reaching the Green Oak, he still couldn't hear any sounds that might betray a pursuer but then the two of them were making so much noise, crashing through the leaves and bracken, all other sounds were smothered.

They were just about to climb over a hedge of creeping shrubs, the only obstacle between them and the safety of the three House Mushrooms, when a loud crack resounded through the clearing. A thick branch on the other side of the low hedge had just been snapped.

The two companions froze in their tracks.

Suddenly, the ground before them erupted into a mountain of churning leaves and dried stems, a monstrous form rose in their path, filling the breeze with streams of leaflitter and twigs. The rising figure seemed to grow forever until it towered above them, claiming them with its awesome shadow. The remnants of its loose Autumnal wrappings peeled away like discarded skin and tumbled back to the floor. The 'thing' slowly brushed the leafy coverings from its huge body; and the bottom half of its massive trunk split into two bulky legs.

Jonquil and Rattajack stared with horror into the face of the largest troll they had ever seen.

It was Ogrod. One of the three Ice Trolls who had borne the sacred Vessels of Light into the Green Sky, he had become separated from the rest of the group and been wandering aimlessly through the forest, desperate for food.

Trolls usually set pretty high standards of ugliness but Jonquil considered this face to be the most grotesque he had ever encountered, what made him look even worse, was the troll's features seemed twisted in confusion. He didn't know quite what to make of the two strange creatures before him. Ogrod lowered his head to try and smell the nature of the two companions and to their ultimate disgust, they felt his hot, rancid breath wash all over them. His face came horribly close and the troll's black, soulless eyes narrowed with ravenous curiosity. His long, scaly tongue snaked out between his swollen lips, tasting the air, then returned to the black cavity between his fat, hanging jowls.

As Ogrod bent lower, thin wisps of matted hair fell across his face and the effort of holding such an uncomfortably stooped position made his breathing deep and laboured; sending oceans of hot stench, ebbing and flowing over the two companions.

Jonquil felt himself being drawn into the troll's vile face as the creature sucked long breaths of air through his cavernous nostrils; but it seemed to the banf the more Ogrod filled his nose with scent, the more confused he became. Finally, he shook his head in violent frustration, growled angrily and revealed a picket fence of ochre teeth behind his drooling lips.

The great troll straightened himself to his full height and tilted his head in puzzlement as he stared down at the two companions. Slowly his hand moved to grasp the hilt of the large axe that hung from his belt, crudely fashioned from a roughly carved boulder and a thick branch. He began to draw the axe from the belt, his eyes never moving, deep creases of confusion still haunting his face.

Jonquil reached out for Rattajack's collar, he had no intention of just standing there waiting to be crushed, it was time for evasive action; with a sudden leap the two of them rushed to the nearest edge of the clearing and dived into the dense bushes. When they turned back to look for the troll the strangest sight greeted them, Ogrod was still staring down at the very spot where the two of them had been

Ogrod, the Ice Troll, roared his annoyance.

Jonquil and Rattajack safe under the eaves of a spreading House Mushroom.

standing. He raised the axe high above his head and with an expectant lick of his lips, brought it whistling down with ground-splitting force. An explosion of leaves and soil filled the air, scattering clouds of brown missiles into the trees and shrubs surrounding the clearing. Then he dropped to his knees with an excited cackle and began raking through the dried layers to find his prey, flinging handfulls of leaf rubbish over his shoulders as he cleaved the ground.

Not being astonishingly bright, Ogrod had excavated quite a crater before he realised his quarry was gone, but by that time it was too late, Jonquil and Rattajack had already crept round to the Green Oak and were safely installed beneath one of the House Mushrooms. Ogrod roared his annoyance and threw great clods of earth at the Green Oak, he swung his axe in furious circles and leapt up and down, stamping both feet hard on the ground like a giant, bad tempered child; but, for all his lack of intelligence, he knew he was beaten.

He slammed the axe hard against his shoulder, turned and stamped sulkily through the trees, in search of easier prey. When the troll turned his back to them, Jonquil noticed some large black patches on his shaggy fur clothing, they were scorch marks and in places the animal hair had been burned down to the skin. Also, the banf noticed that the troll's leggings were badly scratched and torn as if he had been scrambling through thick briars. The troll had the appearance of having recently been in a serious fight, there were thin, red gouges on his arms and neck; and his hair, which would never have been clean or tidy, looked even more bedraggled than usual, it looked as if it had recently been wet.

Jonquil and Rattajack watched the loudly cursing monster disappear into the distance, still a little bemused at their narrow escape. The banf's eyes dropped aimlessly to his legs and then he remembered the Fallon leaves.

In all his fear and surprise he had completely forgotten that the special leaves he wore on his legs and those that he had threaded almost without thinking into Rattajack's collar, had magical powers.

They had found them on one of their adventures, several years before, whilst exploring a distant, little known part of the forest. Growing serenely around a glassy forest pool, they had come across the beautiful Fallon trees, tall and silvery, shimmering with a mystic radiance. Once the leaves had been picked from their boughs they changed to the colour of the soil but mysteriously acquired a most useful gift.

They rendered the wearer invisible, in times of great danger.

Now Jonquil understood. Ogrod had never been able to see them, only smell them, that was what had made him so confused and even though the banf and the terragon had both been invisible, by some strange law they had been able to see each other.

The two companions rested at the Green Oak for as long as they dared and then hurried back to the homeward trail to continue their journey.

The Dragon's Footprint

The afternoon sun speared through the balded branches, casting a spider's web of lace-like patterns across the shadows of the two travellers. A few late butterflies that had been coaxed from hibernation by the rare sunshine, were busy searching for the last drops of precious nectar amongst the flowers of the evergreens.

As they approached the last stretch of their journey, the carpet of dead leaves became far less obstructive and for the first time that day, Jonquil and Rattajack began to make good time.

The gentle warming of the sun on their backs, the familiar sights of home and the fact that they hadn't seen a sign of any other Winter servants, raised their spirits considerably. They climbed the last ridge and there before them, peeping through the wall of trees, was the wonderful sight of The White Ring, less than five hundred paces away.

When Jonquil laid eyes on the row of white mushrooms, a smile broke across his face and he almost laughed with relief. Although a part of him was sad that the last adventure of the year was about to end, secretly he was glad it was all over and that he and his faithful companion had made it back safely to the gates of their kingdom.

It was with a happy spring in their steps that Jonquil and Rattajack neared the white wall.

A hundred paces behind them, peering out at the two companions from amongst the shrubs and evergreens, the warty creature waited patiently. Suddenly, it leapt from its hiding place and ducked inside a concealing hedge of briar patches, it quickly changed its skin to blend perfectly with the bark of the Iron Beech and then bounded from tree to tree, steadily closing on the unsuspecting travellers.

The creature had been stealthily pursuing the banf and the terragon since its first plan of attack had been riotously interrupted by the sudden appearance of the Ice Troll. When the two companions had mysteriously disappeared, the creature thought the troll must have swallowed them whole; and how it had cursed Ogrod under its breath for stealing its meal from it; but then Jonquil and Rattajack had suddenly reappeared beneath the shelter of those nasty mushrooms. The creature knew that the banf-things were slippery but this one and his dragon seemed a particularly artful pair; but, no matter, the creature would get them in the end.

How beautiful the tall, softly translucent mushrooms looked as they loomed before the two companions in the afternoon sun, the threshold of The White Ring stood waiting patiently for them to once again step into its enchanted embrace.

Suddenly something very important happened, which neither of the two returning travellers noticed: Their shadows disappeared. A few seconds later, another one took their place, it was a tall, grotesque shadow, with clawed fingers held aloft. Jonquil and Rattajack turned to face their attacker and gasped in horror at the gargoyle that reached out for them.

The creature's wide, grinning mouth was pulled and distorted by a full armoury of green, slime-stained tusks, its long snout was dominated by large raised nostrils that twitched excitedly. Two prominent bulbous eyes glowed an evil, fiery red and darted to and fro, its domed head was crowned with two curved horns; and a tangled, slimy mane tumbled down the length of its stooped back. The skin of the monster was a mottled riot of bubbling warts that covered its entire body apart from the smooth webs of skin that were stretched between the long, taloned digits of its hands and feet.

It was the Swamp Demon, the legendary bane of the banfs and Jonquil saw that it was every bit as horrific as Old Yargle's tales had described, the terrible creature of myth and fable now stood before them in murderous reality.

The awesome monster snatched at the air around them and began sniffing frantically at the ground, it was then Jonquil realised that the magic of the Fallon leaves had made them invisible again and the creature could only hunt them by scent. They were barely fifty paces from The White Ring, their only chance was to make a dash for it. Before Jonquil could gather enough wits together to grab hold of Rattajack's collar, the terragon seized the end of the banf's cloak in his mouth and dragged him bodily down the path to the white mushrooms. The two companions sprinted for their lives away from the squatting demon and at first it seemed as though they would win but in a moment the creature had overtaken them with a burst of furious leaps and step-hops. Now it blocked their path and they were forced to dive into the cover of the undergrowth at the side of the trail.

The banf and the terragon dodged and twisted through the tangle of stalks and branches in an effort to lose their enemy, they kicked up clouds of leaves and ground rubbish to blind or confuse it, yet the more they tried to thwart the demon, the closer it seemed to follow them.

However they weaved or side-stepped through the trees, the creature was only a breath behind, wherever they ran it scented their trail with frightening speed and accuracy, its eyes may have been no use to it but it could 'see' with its nose.

The Swamp Demon finally seized the exhausted companions less than ten paces from the safety of the white mushrooms, it scooped them up in its webbed hands and held them aloft like two, wriggling trophies. The creature let cry a blood-chilling scream of victory that carried far over the white wall into the kingdom of the banfs. It was also the taunting cry of challenge, for the Swamp Demon wanted the banfs to know that once again it had robbed them; one more of their number had been taken to feed its belly, his faithful dragon to follow; and if any more brave fools dared to venture beyond the magic of The White Ring and trespass in its domain, they too would feel the long fingers of the Swamp Demon around their throat.

Then it was gone, bounding back along the forest trail, its two prizes held high above its head.

The Swamp Demon was only a breath behind.

Jonquil's village was situated only a short distance inside the circle of white mushrooms, the small collection of fungal houses grew amongst the twisted roots of an old Green Oak.

Old Yargle had been quietly dozing on the terrace of his mushroom home, in the warming rays of the afternoon sunshine, when he was suddenly awakened by the terrible scream. He recognised it immediately as the cry of the Swamp Demon and a flood of long-banished memories came rushing back to him.

He remembered the ill-fated adventure he had undertaken with two of his fellows and the terrifying night when the gruesome face of the demon had appeared in the light from their campfire. Old Yargle remembered with shame how he had sat, petrified, whilst his two friends were dragged by their throats into the bushes, never to be seen again. Then that loathsome cry had echoed through the trees; mocking him; humiliating him, daring him to try and rescue his companions if he could find the courage.

When he finally did recover himself and charged through the undergrowth brandishing a burning log, the creature was gone.

At first Old Yargle couldn't understand why he had been spared, perhaps the demon wasn't physically capable of carrying off more than two banfs at a time; but then why hadn't it returned for him later? Eventually the answer came to him, the Swamp Demon was a vain creature and clearly enjoyed his notoriety. Old Yargle had been allowed to return to the Banf Kingdom, in order to tell his people all about the great monster he had encountered beyond The Ring; and so the legend of the Swamp Demon had grown.

The Old One knew that the scream he had heard meant the death of some poor creature, he prayed that it wasn't a banf. He knew Jonquil had not yet returned; because the young adventurer always visited him first to describe in detail the strange sights and wonderful new creatures he and Rattajack had discovered on their travels; and not least to see Old Yargle's beautiful young niece, Meadolarne, who lived in his home with her mother. Meadolarne's father had been one of the two unfortunate banfs who had been taken by the Swamp Demon.

The old banf liked Jonquil, he reminded Old Yargle so much of himself in his younger, exploring days, when he and Chuckwalla, his faithful old terragon, would set out from the Kingdom to explore the lost rivers and deep valleys of the forest.

He prayed the young banf was safe.

The swift moving Swamp Demon carried the two companions far from the brilliant glare of the White Ring. The tall mushrooms burned its eyes when it tried to approach them, as they did all creatures with a black heart. The White Ring had the same punishing effect on the Ice Trolls, hobgoblins and other dark servants that migrated into the Green Sky, with the snow; and although the Swamp Demon, a resident in the great forest, bore no allegiance to the Lord of Winter, it could match the evil of his dark servants measure for measure.

The short, stocky legs of the demon pumped tirelessly along forever changing forest trails, taking the two companions into a region of the Green Sky that was new to them. The failing light of the early evening had an even thicker jungle of tightly packed trees and creepers to battle through before it could make an impression on the gloom of the forest floor.

Despite the dense encroachment of the trees and the snaking progress of the thinning track as it weaved its fragmented way past grotesquely twisted trunks and obtrusive treevines, the Swamp Demon never halted or slowed its pace. It clearly knew this path well.

Jonquil was beginning to feel sea-sick, the erratic lunging of the creature as it jogged and leaped along its winding path, dodging beneath low branches and springing over invasive briars, made the banf's stomach heave and lurch. His arms were clamped tightly by his sides and there was no chance of wriggling free from the monster's iron grip; but, the pressure on his ribs was not as great as it might have been, so Jonquil assumed that the demon wanted them to continue breathing, at least for the time being.

Jonquil's journey was uncomfortable enough but at least he was luckier than Rattajack, somehow the poor terragon had been snatched upside down and his head and forearms were flapping about wildly beneath the demon's tightly clenched grip. Jonquil could not even be sure that his faithful friend was still alive.

The Swamp Demon made little allowance for the thrashing the two companions were suffering from being dragged along the wall of leaves and branches either side of the track. Apart from spitting yet more dead leaves from his mouth, the third occasion that day, Jonquil had even greater discomfort to contend with. His head and neck were a mass of scratches and the supple stems of the evergreens were lashed against his chest and legs with the terrible speed he was thrust at them, even Rattajack's tough, scaly skin revealed traces of branch weals and grazes. Either the Swamp Demon did not care about the injuries he was inflicting on his two captives, or simply did not know, which as they were both still invisible was quite likely.

The wildly twisting forest trail suddenly straightened and ahead of them loomed two enormous Burn-Elders, an extremely unpleasant variety of tree, the trunk of which oozed a slimy, acid-like secretion, that was designed to catch and kill insects which the tree then digested. The huge trees stood like twin sentries guarding the entrance to a forbidden part of the forest. The demon was closing on the narrow gap between them at a terrible pace and Jonquil prayed that there would be sufficient room to save his and Rattajack's skin from the savage trunks as they were carried through.

Just as it was about to leap through the slim gap, the Swamp Demon skidded to a violent halt, almost swinging the two companions on to the burning bark with its momentum. It had clearly been made aware of a strange scent because it began sniffing frantically at the air between the Elders, a large pile of dead leaves had gathered on the far side of the gap and for some reason the creature seemed particularly unsure of it.

Eventually it snorted, made a few encouraging grunts and then tentatively stepped towards the opening, it was impossible to see what lay beyond the two trunks, apart from the fast growing gloom, the trees were far too close together.

Perhaps it was the thought of its home, a dank, seething swamp only a short hop down the trail and the mouth-slavering anticipation of the fresh meal it held in its claws that spurred it on. It gave itself a final reassuring grunt and leapt through the gap, the pile of dry leaves crunching in protest as its webbed foot slapped into the middle of them.

Suddenly the roar of a whiplash cracked against the air and the whole world was turned upside down. The forest floor wheeled backwards and forwards above Jonquil's head, as all three of them spun round in wild, uncontrollable circles, Jonquil's eyes bulged in their sockets and his head buzzed unpleasantly as all his blood rushed downwards.

Rattajack, ironically, was now the right way up and was struggling valiantly to free himself from the demon's still tightly gripped fingers, the monster was not about to surrender its meal that easily.

Jonquil watched in horror as their wild girations swung them dangerously close to the Burn-Elders, the singeing bark missing their skin by a hair's breadth.

The Swamp Demon squirmed and wriggled like a fish on a line to try and free itself from the trap. The loop of rope, that had been cunningly concealed beneath the scattering of dead leaves, drew even tighter around its ankle under the swinging bulk. Every time the demon tried to double up to gnaw at the fibres with its sharp tusks, the struggling weight of its two captives held it down. It couldn't use its hands to free its leg, for fear of losing its meal and the demon couldn't just hang there indefinitely in case the trapper should reappear. It was stalemate.

The more the Swamp Demon angrily wrenched and jerked at the rope, the more painfully it tightened on its leg and consequently the more furious the creature became. The Swamp Demon had just reached the disappointing conclusion that it would have to forego half its meal and release Rattajack to free one of its hands, when the trapper decided to make his appearance. He had been lightly dozing when the trap had sprung and on hearing the loud crack had snatched the axe from his belt and warily moved out from the shadows.

The Swamp Demon shrieked in horror when it saw the approach of the Ice Troll; Ogrod just licked his smiling lips and raised his axe to strike.

The ground suddenly rushed upwards to Jonquil and met violently with his head, as his body fell to earth. Rattajack landed safely on his feet and bounded over to the unconscious banf, grabbed the loose clothing around Jonquil's neck in his mouth and dragged him off down the forest trail.

The Swamp Demon clawed desperately at the rope, after dropping the companions; and he spat curses at the attacking Ice Troll, parried two bone-crunching blows before finally tumbling to freedom. The two fiercesome creatures slowly circled each other, roaring their challenge; and as the lone terragon stumbled down the track, the dead-weight of Jonquil dragging between his legs, bloody battle ensued.

The pool of dry leaves beneath the trap scattered in all directions as the two assailants came together in the shade of the Burn-Elders. The Swamp Demon leapt at the troll and began fiercely raking his chest with its taloned feet. Using its hooked claws it dug into the skin about Ogrod's neck and face, pulling deep trenches across his cheeks. The troll's blood streamed in mingling rivers into the collar of his fur tunic and without reprieve the monster lunged forward to seize his throat in its powerful jaws.

Before the Swamp Demon's cruel tusks could spear the Ice Troll's neck in a vicious death-grip, Ogrod slammed his fist hard into the beast's forehead. The force of the blow launching the demon backwards through the air, tearing large strips of the troll's tunic away with it. Suddenly, a terrible scream tore through the demon's body and Ogrod could just about see, through the bloody, red cloud fogging his vision, that the creature had been thrown on to the searing bark of one of the acid-coated trees.

The Swamp Demon crawled agonizingly away from the Elders, plumes of steam rising angrily from its blistering back. It tried to crawl into the bushes to escape but the troll was upon it, wielding his axe into a whistling blow. Unexpectedly, the demon jumped back to its feet, hurling a handful of leaflitter into the troll's ravaged face. Ogrod's open wounds seethed with pain as they were peppered in grit and his already blood drenched eyes stang in blindness.

Ogrod staggered helplessly back and forth swinging the axe wildly in all directions but to no avail, the demon was careful to stay well back out of harm's way. Then it lunged forward, sinking its razor-like teeth into the troll's weapon-bearing arm, Ogrod roared in pain and the axe fell heavily to the ground. The demon leapt aside as the Ice Troll raged up and down the forest trail in blind panic, punching the air, grasping at any object that came to his waving arms, in a desperate attempt to find his enemy. His staggering feet met with a firm obstruction and he crashed to his knees. The Swamp Demon then withdrew its strategically placed foot and bent to the ground, an evil smile slowly enveloping its face.

Ogrod's eyes cleared just in time to see the Swamp Demon standing before him, the axe being drawn back far over its shoulder and a grin of sheer contempt stretched across its grotesque mouth.

The last thing Ogrod knew was the Demon's ear-piercing cry of triumph as the axe swiftly returned.

In spite of his cumbersome handicap, Rattajack had managed to put quite a reasonable distance between the two of them and the monsters. The victorious roar of the Swamp Demon mixed with the blood-curdling scream of the doomed Ice Troll had urged the terragon's feet to scramble even faster along the stumbling track.

With a terrible fear gripping his heart, Rattajack, galloped through the forest, tripping on roots and boulders, snagging his feet or Jonquil's bouncing body on snatching briars. Suddenly, something heavy crashed into the undergrowth beside him, instinctively he turned to see what it was, almost falling over himself in the process; and the lifeless eyes of Ogrod's disembodied head stared back at him.

The terragon's fearful heart almost burst with shock, his rear legs kicked out in reflex, launching him into the air, his wings spread to ride the breeze and with Jonquil dangling like a puppet from his mouth, the ground fell away beneath them.

Rattajack overcompensated for the banf's swinging weight and dipped at an unexpectedly sharp angle away from the winding trail below. Dusk was rapidly slipping into darkness and the terragon was set the almost impossible task of weaving precariously between the closely grown trunks that raced towards him. Despite his endless difficulties, Rattajack battled valiantly on, carrying them far from the forest path, the Swamp Demon and the place of foul murder.

Eventually sheer physical exhaustion took their toll on the terragon's long neglected flight muscles and he fluttered wearily downwards. The banf's body swaying freely beneath him made landing very complicated and the terragon was not at all sure if he could remember quite how to do it. There was no time for second thoughts as the ground suddenly appeared to claim them, they crashed down a gentle slope of lush grass, tumbling towards their eventual rest amongst a rash of bushy evergreens.

Neither of the two companions were to stir again until morning.

Rattajack awoke with a start. He felt as though he had been asleep for hours and that it must surely be morning but when he opened his eyes the world was till cloaked in darkness. It was strangely silent around him, not even the faintest breeze could be heard brushing against the glossy leaves of the evergreens; and yet there was a sound. A strange, rasping sound that seemed to emanate from quite close to him, almost echoing around his head as though he were in a cave. It was a deep, rhythmic sound, growing and fading with certain regularity, hoarse and hollow. The terragon lowered an investigative ear towards the sleeping banf and the mystery was solved, it was Jonquil's breathing, long and drawn out from the depths of slumber.

Rattajack tentatively edged forward, the branches of the thick evergreen bush scraped along his scaly flanks as he tunnelled through, then the terragon's nose met with a solid wall. It was icy cold and its texture was rough and powdery. Rattajack pushed his nose at the substance and it yielded, when he withdrew, a slight amount of creamy light glowed from the centre of the impression. He decided to use the arrow at the end of his tail to excavate the freezing wall, rather than his sensitive nose. To do this required a spot of tight manoeuvring in the cramped conditions and as he knocked the stems of the plants around him, tiny showers of ice crystals trickled down from above, whispering through the layers of shiny foliage.

The glowing wall creaked and groaned as the terragon's tail burrowed through; and then suddenly a whole section crumbled away, allowing dazzling beams of daylight to burst in upon their twilight world beneath the evergreens. Rattajack squinted painfully as a blinding sea of brightness invaded his eyes, the subdued tones of the Autumn forest were gone, a dramatic transformation had taken place; the world was white.

The terragon pushed his way through the remaining obstruction, a gasp steaming into the sharp air as he blinked at the changed forest. The snowfall had been surprisingly deep. The bower of dense evergreens in which they had slept and had been completely covered, creating a sealed cocoon around them. The snow was piled in thick ledges along the wind-stripped branches that criss-crossed above Rattajack's head and the rolling bank of lush grass down which they had violently arrived the night before was now smothered in a pristine white blanket. It looked as though a whole Winter's worth of snow had fallen during their sleeping hours; but hovering above the forest, bursting with menace, the sullen clouds in the sky promised a lot more to come.

Rattajack crunched back to the evergreen cave where Jonquil lay, the banf was still fast asleep.

The white bank above the bushes looked very inviting, the terragon had always loved the snow and even though it wasn't the time or the place for fun and games, Rattajack decided there would be no harm in just one long slide; whilst he was waiting for Jonquil to wake. He looked in on the banf one final time to make sure he was alright and then began the long trudge up to the summit of the slope, the depth of the snow making him pant with the effort. By the time he had struggled to the top, long plumes of steam were spewing out from his gaping mouth and the terragon began to wonder at the wisdom of such an energy-wasting climb, his goal achieved, he slumped into the snow, exhausted.

Then he saw it, an incredible vision through the trees, a multicoloured jewel set in the endless white world. A sheer impossibility, an illusion; and yet there it was. Rattajack launched himself down the crisp run of snow, ploughing through the virginal covering, scattering tiny white fragments that grew into small spheres as they tumbled down the slope. After carving a wavering furrow in the bank, the terragon bounded off through the creaking snow to investigate.

Whilst Rattajack went off to explore, Jonquil groaned his way back to consciousness. His head pounded like thunder and his body felt as though it had been lashed to wooden poles and severely beaten. When he finally gathered enough courage to venture sitting up, the Pain Demons began to beat a jungle rhythm on his temples with stone mallets.

'Rattajack' he breathed, even a whisper tore through his senses. Jonquil could only bear to open his eyes a tiny amount and grimaced at the hole of light illuminating their sleeping place; the terragon was gone. The banf squinted through a fence of dark eyelashes and tried to identify exactly where he was. He groped along the crusty ground between the thick stems of the evergreen bushes, his fingers found a sideways growing branch and he pulled at it to try and lever himself upwards. Suddenly, a large wedge of snow was loosened from above and it crashed on to his head most of it sliding down the back of his neck. He cried out in shock and frantically pulled at the bottom of his shirt to allow the freezing fragments to escape, bouncing against the ground to shake them out. By the time he had finished, he was exhausted, wet; and even more miserable; the Pain Demons had now migrated from their feverish work at his temples and were galloping up and down his bruised body. Jonquil crawled towards the light, his eyes stinging with its intensity, then his narrowed gaze fell on the frozen forest and his heart sank.

The treacherous Lord of Winter had cast his great white net over the world; and they were caught. The first snows had arrived and with them, no doubt, countless blood-thirsty, murder-loving, ice monsters. Jonquil wondered if they would ever see their home again.

For a moment despair gripped him and his face fell into the crispy bedding. He didn't know where he was, he didn't know where Rattajack was; and every time he tried to remember what had happened after they had been caught in the Ice Troll's trap, his head ached in protest.

Then a cold, wet snout nuzzled his ear and his face lifted; the terragon had returned. His eyes were bright with excitement and with a slowly dawning dread Jonquil recognised the urgent, 'follow me' expression beamed across the terragon's face. He pushed Rattajack away with a murmured grumble and curled up to sleep off his suffering; the terragon was having none of it, he snapped his jaws on to the collar of Jonquil's cloak and with an obstinate determination hauled him out through the snow-hole. The banf picked himself up out of the trench he had just violently ploughed, coughing and spitting out lumps of snow; Rattajack piped at him imploringly, grabbing the hem of his cloak and pulling him forward. Jonquil snatched the material back from the terragon's jaws, growling miserably at him; and held the sides of his head in dreaded anticipation of the whiplash of pain his sudden movements would have caused. To his pleasant surprise, no such agonizing retribution materialised, in fact the vigorous dousing in the snow seemed to have cleared his head considerably; and even revived his aching body a little.

He apologised to the excited terragon for his sharp words and at Rattajack's energetic insistence, the two of them trudged off through the snow, retracing the terragon's earlier steps, to see his discovery; so exciting that it could not wait.

When they arrived at the place, Jonquil almost dropped to his knees in amazement at what he saw, his mouth had already fallen open and his sleepy eyes were stretched into wide, awe-struck circles.

Before them was a forest pool, which should have been glazed over with thick, grey ice and buried beneath a liberal dumping of snow, the trees and bushes around the pool were still deeply clothed in the white garments of Winter; but the water and its surrounding banks were an oasis of intense greenery and colour, throbbing with life and activity.

Clouds of mosquitos danced and spiralled above the slightly steaming surface of the water; small fish darted nervously to and fro in the crystal clear depths, occasionally diving for shelter into the thick, emerald plaits of pondweed that formed luxuriant swirling meadows on the gravelly bottom. A flash of azure. A fabulous dragonfly swept through the mist of hovering insects; there were more, sparkling emerald and bronze. They would land on one of the lily pads that were spotted numerously about the pond and spar valiantly with their rivals; flashing iridescent crystal wings.

The sun seemed to favour this enchanted scene and gazed down on it with unseasonal warmth; frogs basked in its welcome attention, perfectly camouflaged against a mossy log or decaying lily pad. A small collection of forest birds had been attracted and hopped through the green branches overhanging the water, singing full-throated songs in praise of the miracle.

The banks of the pool were adorned in a riot of flowers. Some crept down to the water's edge in long, delicate tresses, bright yellow florets studded along their stems. There were carpets of delicate blues and violets; golden stars that burst forth from round,shiny leaves covering the ground. Eruptions of ruby-red blooms held aloft on towering purple spikes marched up the slope away from the water, mingling with tall flowering herbs, radiant in exotic shades.

The bright splashes of colour were not confined to the land, the shallow margins were graced with a glittering array of surface floating plants in full blossom, exquisite clusters of white and gold cups raised their heads above the glassy surface; and in the deeper shallows, the magnificent water-lily flowers, in glorious hues of white, red and purple, sat on the water in breath-taking, star-like perfection: jewels of the night, stolen from heaven.

All of the blooms on or around the pond pulsated with the feverish attentions of bees and other nectar-seeking insects, gathering their sweet plunder in frenzied haste, lest the miracle should fade; and the cruel Winter rush back in.

At the far side of the pond, an ancient, thick-set willow was growing, its tangled roots arching into the water from the bank like a twisted cage. Its foliage, which looked remarkably dense and lush, only flourished on the side of the trunk that faced the pool, the other side was bare and burdened with snow. The leaves of the willow were so thick and dark in places that they completely obscured its weeping boughs; casting a dominant shadow over the breeze-rippled margins.

The strange enchantment that radiated from the pool had pushed back the snow to a severe line above the flourishing banks, white against green. The forest pool was caught in the spell of Summer and wherever the power emanated from, it drove back the force of Winter and created an island of warmth and light in a sea of cold darkness.

Jonquil was mesmerised by the brightly coloured spectacle, a richly patterned butterfly fluttered into his face and after investigating him at close quarters, continued disinterested on the breeze. The banf could hear the rhythmic chatter of grasshoppers and crickets rattling in the long grass, their abrasive conversations carrying across the water to each other in the bright sunshine. The plop of a large fish caused golden rings to grow across the pool, the water gently undulating into the armies of tall reeds; and tiny, unseen creatures squeaked and mewed as they chased each other through the extravagant undergrowth.

Jonquil and Rattajack stepped across the border between Winter and Summer and immediately the air felt warmer, they waded through the tall, flowering stems, inhabited by jumping insects and industrious, brightly coloured beetles; and carefully trod through an orgy of blossoms to make their way down to the soft earth by the water's edge.

The banf cautiously tasted the water, it was delicious; Rattajack was already gulping great mouthfuls, his body half submerged. The two companions suddenly discovered a long neglected thirst and drank eagerly. When they had finally quenched themselves their thoughts turned to food; they hadn't eaten anything for a whole day, since the sumptuous meal of Fallen Star the morning before. Jonquil looked hopefully at the banks around him for something to eat and began foraging through the long grass for small mushrooms, Rattajack had decided to forget his appetite for a while and take to the water.

Jonquil was just about to warn the terragon not to make too much noise and to keep on his guard when Rattajack squirted a long jet of water full into his face, the banf's words emerged as an incomprehensible jumble of gurgles. Before he had time to recover, the terragon artfully skimmed his tail spear across the top of the water, drenching Jonquil with one, sweeping blow.

'Right!' Jonquil roared, completely forgetting the need for silence, 'You have done it now!' Before his feet could splash through the shallows in pursuit, Rattajack had already swum out into the deeper water and dived beneath the sun-sparkled surface. Jonquil could hardly run for laughing and he thrashed fistfuls of spray in the vague direction of the terragon before finally losing his feet and crashing under the water. He was thoroughly soaked now so there was no reason not to go further and follow Rattajack into the crystal depths. The banf could see the terragon weaving gracefully through the long strands of pondweed like a true aquatic creature, he was a perfect swimmer, moving effortlessly through the water, only betraying himself with the occasional string of bubbles. Then he was gone, his body wriggling like an eel through the submerged forest, until only his waving tail could be seen and then it too disappeared.

Jonquil was standing waist deep in the pool, searching the shimmering green depths for his companion's reappearance, the sunlight was reflected on to the gravel at the bottom in dancing white lines, that shattered into a frenzy of spinning fragments when he drew his fingers across the water's skin. A school of tiny fish playing follow the leader, swam quite close to him and then shot away in an exploding silver shower when he tried to touch them; Jonquil looked for clues over the surface of the pond to locate the terragon; and his eyes were drawn by a sapphire dragonfly tracing a golden thread across the dark glassy reflection of the willow tree.

A chain of silvery bubbles appeared in a wide arc off to the side, the banf didn't see them and two long, pointed ears slowly rose from the water behind him. Jonquil moved a little closer to the growth of underwater plants and tried to peer into their thick mass, he was growing a little concerned, Rattajack had been down there a long while, suddenly a clump of slimy pondweed slapped on to the back of his neck and when he turned round another jet of water spurted into his face. The terragon stayed surfaced long enough to chirrup a chorus of cheeky notes and then disappeared once more from view, with a final flick of his tail. Jonquil decided to leave the pool to Rattajack and waded back to the bank to dry himself out.

The terragon was a joy to watch, twisting and turning, diving to play tag with the large fish through the tangled stems of pondweed, he almost looked as though he belonged in the water, as if it might truly be his natural state.

Jonquil could only guess that the great affinity all terragons seemed to have with water of any description, pools, rivers, streams; was closely related to the nature of their birth, which took place on the water.

Terragons were born from special hatching buds that rose to the surface, from eggs buried in the sandy bottom. As soon as the baby terragons burst through the petals of the floating buds they cried out for their mothers. The she-terragons, who would have been waiting for days on the banks of the hatching pool to greet their only offspring, would pipe calls of encouragement to their little one, coaxing it to climb out of the bud and swim its way to shore.

Jonquil had not been able to be present at Rattajack's birth because the banf and terragon were both born at exactly the same time, a rare event in the banf kingdom; but one which always resulted in the two companions being inseparable for life; as Jonquil and Rattajack undoubtedly were.

Jonquil did remember, however, witnessing the birth of his cousin's terragon, Snappa. Baby terragons were even more mischievous than their fully grown elders, if such a thing was possible; and Snappa had poked his nose in to everything. He'd broken in to cousin Peeli's food chamber and experienced his first feast by devouring a whole, delicious Fallen Star that his master had been saving for a birthday banquet; he had also taken a distinct liking for chewing the end of Chuckwalla's tail, much to the annoyance of the older terragon; and only desisted when Rattajack grudgingly parted with one of his treevine collars for the baby terragon to try his jaws on that. Snappa had developed two passions: mushrooms and snow. The former he loved to eat, climb and sleep under and the latter he loved to leap and frolic in. When, one Winter's morning, Rattajack's favourite vine ball went missing, a brief exploration of the trees around the village, revealed the tiny terragon gambolling through the snow in wild, ecstatic circles, chasing the ball, which was almost as big as himself, around the tall trunks.

For one gloomy moment, Jonquil wondered if they would ever laugh with the likes of Snappa, Chuckwalla, Peeli and their other friends and family in the banf kingdom again. Rattajack was still splashing and diving in the clear water, carefree and oblivious, Jonquil had almost dried completely in the warm sun and decided to explore the margins of the pool, hoping to find a clue to its strange power; or at the very least, something to eat.

A little way along the bank, he came to a dense growth of reeds, growing out into the water; he had to battle his way through them to reach the soft, damp ground on the other side. When he finally emerged, plucking a few persistent reed burs from his hair and clothes, the sight that greeted him chilled his heart, and made his eyes grow wide with fear.

Pressed into the soft earth by the water's edge was a massive footprint, a giant's stride away there was another; and in between there was one much less significant impression, obviously made by a smaller limb. The huge prints had three forward pointing toes and one rear, the ends of the digits were clearly armed with powerful claws. The first thought to shoot into Jonquil's mind on seeing the footprints was the Swamp Demon, perhaps it had followed them and secretly slipped into the water whilst they played; with all the commotion they had kicked up, neither of them would have noticed; but, then after the banf had calmed a little, he realised that the prints were leading away from the pool, not towards it and the mystery creature clearly did not possess webbed feet. Whatever it was that had made the fearful impressions it must have visited the pool before they arrived; after all, in

Snappa, the baby terragon, had poked his nose into everything.

Jonquil placed his foot into the giant footprint.

that ageless place where time seemed to play no part, everything stayed fresh forever; and the prints could have been made weeks before. Although with the mean dose of good fortune they had received so far on this trip, a niggling voice at the back of Jonquil's mind told him, the chances were, it would not be so.

Jonquil stepped out of the reeds, across a small carpet of flat green leaves and placed his foot reverently into the giant footprint. The Ice Troll had towered above him and made him feel small, the Swamp Demon had held him aloft like a babe in arms and made him feel weak and insignificant; but the awesome spread of the gargantuan impression surrounding his foot, suddenly made him feel as tiny and as vulnerable as a beetle in the grass. He could only hope that the owner of the footprint was many days distant, just a lasting memory in the preserving soil of the Summer pool.

Treasures to be Found

Jonquil climbed the flower studded bank to scour the surrounding snowy trees for signs of the mystery beast; the stark branches cast pale, blue-ish shadows on the endless white carpet: but the snow was undisturbed, there was no trail; the creature had clearly departed before the heavy snowfall.

The banf was just about to return to the poolside to give Rattajack the unwelcome news that it was time to leave, when a bold reflection, in the heart of the deep water, caught his eye. At first he thought it was only a ripple, glancing a shard of sunlight as it glided across the surface; but when he looked again, it remained, constant, unmoving; and Jonquil realised that the reflection was not on the top of the water but some distance beneath it.

'It's probably just a dead fish lying on the bottom,' he told himself, 'Its shiny flank catching the sun.' However, anything being allowed to die in that enchanted place seemed quite unthinkable, if not impossible; he was convinced the sharp glimmer was something more.

The reflection was not so easily seen from the water's edge, which would explain why neither he nor Rattajack had noticed it before. After Jonquil had called the playful terragon to attention, he waded out towards the depths; Rattajack greeted him by swirling around his body in excited circles and then his happy face bobbed up beside him, to listen to the banf's instructions.

Jonquil was standing neck-deep in the water, the forest of matted pondweed lay before him and somewhere in the middle of it was the shining, golden thing, he had seen from the top of the bank; it was very likely that the terragon had discovered it already, in the course of his aquatic games, so it was probably nothing exciting.

Following a furious bout of swimming actions and downward pointing by the banf, Rattajack uptailed and slipped gracefully into the submerged garden; a few eruptive bubble bursts later, the terragon eventually re-emerged, breathless and gasping to fill his lungs with air.

'What's wrong, Ratters?' Jonquil asked in a whisper, for some strange reason suddenly feeling the need to be quiet and secretive. Rattajack gave a little whimper; and wore a slightly troubled expression on his face; then he arched into the air once more and disappeared beneath a brief rise of white water. Another succession of silvery bubbles snaked out from among the weeds; and this time the wrestling form of the terragon appeared between the tall, wagging stems: urging a large, dark object into the open. Long strands of weed floated to the surface as they were dislodged by the dark shape, dragging along the bottom; and when Rattajack abandoned his work to refill his lungs, the sun reached through the clouded water and revealed a whole display of golden adornments on the object's body.

To drag their find into the shallows took every ounce of strength the two of them could muster; it had a geometric, regimented shape that resisted the water, making movement difficult.

The chest was covered in a tangle of curly pondweed and green algae; and the two companions carefully stripped all the slimy wrappings from its beautifully decorated form. The arched lid of the chest was richly inlaid with fabulous scrolls and fretwork in solid gold; there were also exquisite panels fashioned into its surface, portraying delicate florals representing the blooms of the season. The side panels of the chest were cleaned to reveal breathtaking arrangements of jewelled flowers, set in even more precious metal, blossoming in skilfully designed splendour; casting floral shaped reflections on the wet faces of the two companions as they knelt close to admire them.

Jonquil had never seen anything so beautiful in his life. The richness and the artistry of the priceless creation raised a rash of goose-pimples on the back of his neck. The chest spoke of a world beyond his imagination; a land of wondrous cities and peoples, his wanderer's soul ached to see: a land far from the eaves of the Green Sky Forest, the only world he had ever known.

Jonquil raised the lid; and was hardly surprised to see the chest full to the brim with greenish, muddy water. When the lid was eased back, a magnificent jewelled dragon seized the dazzling sunlight and returned it as a thousand radiant stars, the incredible beast soared across the roof of the chest in full majestic flight; ruby studded fire spewing from its snarling jaws.

'One of your big cousins, eh Ratters?' Jonquil teased, Rattajack nodded in mesmerised acquiescence. The terragon was clearly affected by the striking image portrayed before him; his eyes burned with wonder as they followed the sweeping form of the great dragon across the lid; he was a prince; and the terragon felt humble to be bathed in his reflection.

The banf tipped the chest on to its side; and the muddy contents spilled into the shallows. Once it had been righted again, they could see the walls of the chest inside. Originally they had been lined in the finest golden velvet; but now it was ripped and stained; and there were, tiny, wormy creatures wriggling across the torn pieces. Lying ominously in the bottom, covered in a thick coating of green slime, were two large boulders.

'Who would want to sink such a beautiful object?' Jonquil gasped. Apart from the slight soiling inside, the chest was in excellent condition. The banf was not at all sure what material it was constructed from; he could only guess that it was a highly decorative form of wood or similarly light substance; otherwise, why the need for two heavy stones to weigh it down?

Jonquil stepped back from the chest and gave it a long, thoughtful look.

'I wonder how long it has been down there,' he finally said. He continued to stare dreamily at the chest, whilst Rattajack sniffed around the fascinating object, examining every inch in the closest detail. The two companions were so engrossed in their precious discovery, both equally hypnotised by its shimmering radiance; that neither of them saw the old willow tree on the far side of the pool begin to change.

Dark patches of foliage became walls of armoured scales, slowly unravelling from the arched branches in thick slithering coils. Most of the tree's mass gently migrated groundwards, a huge form twisting in descent around the wizened trunk; sliding coils releasing the bared branches in retreating spirals. As the great body neared the ground, limbs, armed with hooked, ivory talons, hugged the ancient bark; leathery wings lay neatly in their resting place like folded, ship's sails, a long prehensile tail snaked upwards into the tree in tight circles.

When the first clawed foot touched the ground, a terrible head swept round from the other side of the tree; its fierce, blood-chilling eyes watching with cool interest, the activities of the two companions across the water.

The rows of steely scales on the greater part of its arched body had blended perfectly with the yellowy leaf spears that foliaged the willow; but once the creature had fully descended and the sun was allowed to play across its layered covering; its tough skin became a blaze of shimmering golden hues, the scales reflecting a celebration of the richest shades of Summer.

The dragon's head was a forest of cruel, curving antlers, set upon a long, sweeping bronze throat, armies of ivory daggers bristled inside his powerful rock-breaking jaws; and his keen eyes narrowed in estimation of the two figures in the far shallows.

Rattajack's head lifted suddenly, a strange awareness overcame him; and he slowly turned to look into the eyes of the golden dragon. The terragon gasped in awe; he recognised him as the dragon portrayed in the chest; only the original was infinitely more impressive than his jewelled picture. Like the image in the chest, however, the dragon was both terrifying and aristocratic; he had a noble bearing and a dignified, arrogant air. Rattajack had been right, the dragon was a prince.

The great head lowered slowly to the water's edge and as he sipped from the pool, soft plumes of steam rose lazily from his nostrils, the dragon fully lifted his head again and the water flowed in rhythmic ripples down his long, slender throat. Then he spoke to the two companions, his voice booming across to them in deep, gravelly tones.

'I am Arangast,' he said, 'Guardian of the Summer Vessel.'

Jonquil, who had been squatted with his back to the dragon, closely examining the finely detailed workmanship of the chest's outside walls, suddenly spun around. He was so surprised at seeing the terrifying vision before him, he staggered back into the chest, completely lost his balance, tipped over and crashed into the muddy shallows on the other side. Eventually two fearful, green eyes, set in a dripping, dirt-streaked face, peeped over the top of the chest at the mighty dragon.

'You need not fear me, little one,' the dragon said to him, 'I have no will to harm you.'

'Where did *you* come from?' The banf asked.

'I was in the tree. I have been watching you from the very first moment you arrived here.' The dragon replied.

A slight twinge of embarrassment coloured Jonquil's cheeks, he thought of all the silly horseplay they had indulged in, splashing around like two mad things;

hurling great clumps of weed at each other. What must the dragon have thought of them? Rattajack did not look the least bit embarrassed, he was just staring ahead, dumbstruck; silenced with awe and wonder.

'What do you want with us?' Jonquil asked.

'First, I should thank you.'

'Thank us?'

'For retrieving the Sacred Vessel from the water,' the dragon told him.

'This beautiful chest is yours?' asked the banf.

'Not mine,' the dragon replied 'but it is my duty to guard it.'

Jonquil could not decide whether they should trust the dragon or not. He might simply have been keeping the two of them talking whilst he slowly manoeuvred himself into a better position to strike; but then, the chest was extraordinarily rich and beautiful; and if it belonged to the banf, would he not set a magnificent dragon to guard it? But then why had it been languishing at the bottom of an enchanted forest pool, with two large boulders inside it? Suddenly the whole thing had become very mysterious. Then the banf realised something, which should have occurred to him the moment the golden dragon addressed him directly. He was visible. The Fallon leaves hadn't made him disappear; this meant that either all the splashing about in the water had washed the magic from them, or he was not in any danger from the dragon.

'Allow me to introduce myself again,' the dragon said courteously, 'I am Arangast, Guardian of the Sacred Vessel of Summer. Which, of course, is the precious article you see before you.'

Feeling a little braver, Jonquil climbed to his feet and stepped out from behind the chest. Despite his mud-stained, dishevelled appearance, the banf felt honour-bound to show a mark of respect to Arangast; and as much to please Rattajack, who was now looking at him expectantly, as anything else. He took a step towards the dragon and bowed deeply.

'Sir!' he said, for want of a better word, not really knowing the correct protocol when addressing a noble dragon. To Jonquil's utter amazement, Arangast did likewise, to both of them. Rattajack piped appreciatively.

'You are not a goblin,' the dragon stated, almost as if Jonquil was not aware of the fact that this was so.

'Most certainly not,' the banf confirmed.

'You are not a man.'

'Er . . . no!' Jonquil replied, not absolutely sure what a man was.

'An elf, perhaps?' the dragon continued.

'Again, no. I am a banf,' he said proudly.

'The name is vaguely familiar to me,' Arangast said uncertainly, trying not to cause Jonquil any offence.

'We are the forest people,' the banf told him. 'The Green Sky Forest is our home We live within the boundary of the White Ring, in the Banf Kingdom, it's not too far away from here; somewhere over the . . .' Suddenly, Jonquil realised that he had no idea in which direction the Banf Kingdom lay, since their adventures with

"I am Arangast, Guardian of the Summer Vessel."

the Ice Troll and the Swamp Demon, they had become totally lost. He quickly changed the subject.

'Er . . . I am called Jonquil, Jonquil the Wanderer; and this is . . .

'Rattajack,' Arangast interrupted. 'I know, we have already spoken.'

Jonquil was mystified.

'But how . . . ?'

This time is was Arangast's turn to change the subject.

'Was the Sacred Vessel difficult to move? I should imagine for someone of your size, it would be very heavy,' the dragon said.

'It was,' Jonquil replied, 'But I'm afraid Rattajack did most of the work. He's a much stronger swimmer than I am. Did you cast the chest into the water?'

'No!'

'Then who did?' Jonquil asked.

A deep growl preceded the dragon's answer but finally he spat the words out. 'The enemy!'

Jonquil felt sure he ought to be impressed by Arangast's answer; but unfortunately the dragon's words meant nothing to him.

'What enemy?'

Arangast gave the banf a slightly disbelieving, sideways glance.

'Are you serious?' he asked incredulously.

'Of course,' Jonquil replied.

The golden dragon looked decidedly bemused.

'You mean to say, you know nothing of the Ice Sorcerer, or the Grand Betrayal, or the stealing of the Sacred Vessels?' he asked.

'I'm afraid I don't,' Jonquil answered.

'You know nothing of what has happened in the outside world in recent days?'

'We have never seen the outside, up to yet,' Jonquil began, 'It's so far away; but we hope to some day.'

'Most baffling!' Arangast sighed. 'I was not prepared for this!'

Jonquil offered another question.

'Do the Winter trolls and goblins have anything to do with the enemy?'

'Most assuredly!' Arangast exclaimed.

'Oh, well,' Jonquil continued, casually seating himself on the closed lid of the priceless chest.

'We know of them.'

The banf then proceeded to tell the golden dragon all about Ogrod, the Swamp Demon and the terrifying events of the day before. He became a little vague when he got to their escape from Ogrod's rope trap; and waking up in the snow-cocooned evergreen bush; but, the dragon seemed to be following remarkably well: and even nodded in agreement at some of Jonquil's conclusions. By the time the banf had finished telling his story, he had the mysterious feeling that the dragon had heard it somewhere before; and as impossible as it seemed, somehow knew more about their adventures than Jonquil did. Before he had time to dwell on these thoughts for too long, Arangast spoke.

'The two of you have indeed experienced a great adventure,' he began, 'But now, allow me to tell *you* a tale. A tale of the outside world. A tale of treachery and evil, of powers and destruction so dark, they will chill your heart.'

Jonquil's eyes shone with excitement, he always loved to hear talk of the outside world; and although so few banfs in the kingdom could claim any knowledge of such matters, he always listened intently when old adventurers such as Yargle or Targrin told about their bold escapades on the sweeping green plains beyond the forest.

The young banf sat patiently on the chest whilst Arangast told him about Vrorst's treachery and the plight of the three wizards. How he and his brothers had been released from the Sacred Chamber to seek their precious charges; and how Arangast had been drawn to the Summer chest by its own inherent power.

'But why didn't you try to rescue the chest yourself?' Jonquil asked him.

'I was afraid to,' Arangast rather shamefully admitted. 'The Vessels are so valuable, so delicate. If I tried to lift it from the pool with my teeth or my claws, I would surely have damaged it. I dared not take the risk.'

'So, you simply climbed into the tree and decided to wait for help to arrive,' Jonquil stated.

'I had no other choice,' Arangast claimed, 'What else could I do?'

'But how did you know that we were not part of the enemy?' Jonquil asked.

'At first, I did not,' The dragon began, 'So I waited. Then when you began laughing and playing in the water, your voices drenched with happiness, I knew you could not be from Vrorst. His servants are foul, spiteful creatures, whose harsh laughter only rings out with greed or evil deeds. I knew that it was only a matter of time before someone was attracted by the Summer Vessel's spell.'

'You are lucky it was not the Ice Troll!' Jonquil told him.

'Lucky! Pah!' The dragon pursed his lips in disgust and spat a jet of real fire into the pool, a burst of steam erupted angrily from the water.

'If that evil cur had dared to show his face again, I would have ripped him in two!' As Arangast growled his words across the pool, his spear sharp talons tore into the bank beneath him, ploughing destructive furrows into the beds of Summer flowers.

'I followed the progress of the Sacred Vessel in the hands of the enemy; then suddenly, I came upon them. They scattered before me like leaves in the wind, such is the bravery of the dark servants. They all fled but one, he was the Ice Troll burdened with the Vessel. He took fright when he saw me and tried to escape through the thick undergrowth; but he was slow and stumbling. Eventually he staggered here to the forest pool, it was dull and lifeless; and in his panic he seized two boulders from the bank, threw them roughly into the Vessel and then hurled it into the deep waters.

Although I was horrified at his actions; once he had given up possession of the Sacred Vessel, I was able to attack him. I had not dared to do so before, for fear of causing damage to the precious object. My intention was to roast him alive for his evil part in the grand treachery; but he foiled me. As soon as I sprayed him in flame he dived into the pool, dousing my fire. He was able to swim a lot better than I assumed; and to my shame, he escaped me; but it is gratifying to learn that the evil creature did not live long; and was soon to meet a violent end at the hands of the Swamp Demon.'

'He did?' Jonquil interrupted, 'How do you know that?'

The dragon did not answer but stared emphatically at Rattajack. Jonquil followed his eyes to the terragon; but Rattajack just gazed back at him innocently. The banf was rapidly beginning to understand the full extent of his companion's special senses, he was clearly able to communicate with the dragon by some, unseen, unheard language.

'So, the troll was killed, eh Ratters?'

The terragon piped in agreement.

'Then what happened to the Swamp Demon?' he asked.

Rattajack turned to Arangast and began to stare hypnotically into the golden dragon's eyes. Occasionally an ear would twitch or one of his feet slap the ground, almost to accentuate his silent speech. Eventually, Arangast turned to Jonquil and repeated in the spoken tongue, everything that had happened to the two companions after the death of the Ice Troll. Jonquil could not decide which it was that astounded him more; finding out that he and Rattajack had flown through the trees, or that his terragon companion had a new trick. Telepathy with dragons.

'What are you going to do now?' Jonquil finally asked Arangast.

'I must return the Sacred Vessel to my Lord Orolan,' the dragon replied.

'But what of the other chests, I mean, Vessels,' Jonquil continued, 'How will your brother dragons recover theirs without any help?'

'Perhaps they too will meet two friendly travellers,' Arangast offered.

'Not now the snows have fallen, they won't. The only travellers that walk in the forest at this time of year, are those that have travelled from the far north, the creatures of Winter!' the banf exclaimed.

The dragon considered for an instant; his orders had been to seek out and recover the Summer Vessel, no mention had been made of aiding his brother Guardians; but then, what use was just one Vessel being returned to the wizards, when they needed all three?

'Jonquil the Wanderer,' he said, 'You are right, I should help my brothers and I am ashamed that I did not propose it; but you and Rattajack have risked your lives enough, let me escort you back to your kingdom and safety.'

'No, there is no time!' Jonquil protested, 'Rattajack and I are the only friendly faces you are likely to find, this side of the White Ring, to help you in your quest. Now the snows have fallen, the Green Sky will soon become the home to marauding armies of Ice Trolls, Hobgoblins and the rest. When they discover that the sacred chests are working magic around themselves, revealing their hiding places. I'll wager, the foul creatures that stole the Vessels in the first place, will return to steal them again; perhaps even to destroy them! By the way you described them, Arangast, they seem the sort of devils who would resort to anything, rather than let the three wizards take the Vessels back.'

The golden dragon hung his head, he knew it was the truth.

'You are right,' he said, 'And I am deeply indebted to you both.'

'Then let us depart as soon as possible,' Jonquil began 'Do you know where we may find the other Sacred Vessels?'

'My brother Guardians and I, were convinced that all three Vessels were brought into this great forest for concealment. The Ice Sorcerer's servants simply would not have had time to find a better hiding place,' the dragon explained.

'Believe me, Arangast,' Jonquil told him, 'The Green Sky Forest is good enough! We have no small task ahead of us!'

So it was that Jonquil and Rattajack, no longer simple adventurers, were swept up in the great wave of high sorcery that was breaking over the land.

The two companions dragged the chest on to the bank; and finished cleaning its decorated surfaces. Then they attended to themselves, Jonquil had a head caked in mud to wash out; and Rattajack just thought he would splash around in the water a little longer, to keep the banf company. Jonquil pulled the treevine collar over the terragon's head and wrung it free of water, Rattajack then trotted on to the dry ground on the bank; and spun around in wild circles, trying to catch his tail, the instinctive method all terragons used to dry their skin. A shower of speeding water droplets were flung from his spinning body; and by the time he had finished, Jonquil, who had been unwisely standing nearby, needed to dry himself off all over again. Arangast, who stood by, patiently waiting for them, could not help smiling at the antics of his new found friends. Jonquil's protests, as he began to rub himself down again, with his shoulder-cloak, after Rattajack had sprayed him with water: the brief bout of comic wrestling that was required to push the collar back over the terragon's head, which ended in the two companions both collapsing in an hysterical heap.

Eventually they were ready; and the Sacred Vessel was strapped, rather unceremoniously, to the dragon's back, using fresh treevines from the old willow. Jonquil and Rattajack were persuaded by Arangast, to climb up with the chest; and when all was secure, the three of them set off into the trees.

With its heart removed, the spell over the forest pool was broken; and the colourful oasis began to wither and die. Fingers of ice crept out across the still surface of the water, the exquisite flowers shrivelled in the biting wind, the bees and insects fled for their lives. In a short while the pool was frozen; and its flourishing banks were frost-burned, wilted and desolate.

The three travellers had no idea in which direction the other two Sacred Vessels lay, the sweeping expanse of the great Green Sky Forest stretched before them, offering a myriad of twisting forest trails for them to follow. At first, the dragon took them in a series of wide, aimless circles, picking any winding track that looked vaguely hopeful; but the only traces that marked the deep snow, were those made by the forest game or birds. They had searched for most of the day before any positive clues crossed their path.

Jonquil had just wrenched a large bracket fungus from the bark of an Iron Beech as they passed by, to make a long awaited meal for himself and Rattajack; when

Arangast spotted a line of heavy tracks up ahead, bursting through the wall of undergrowth on to the trail. When they reached the place where the creature had broken through, the three travellers could see that a few thick branches had been hacked asunder by some crude implement; and left strewn in the snow. Rattajack communicated to Arangast, who in turn informed the banf, that the scent hanging in the air around the forced opening, smelled strongly of the enemy. They could see by the size and depth of the tracks, that the creature was much larger than a hobgoblin, it was probably an Ice Troll, one of Ogrod's ugly relatives; and very likely of equal size and stature. Jonquil suddenly had an extremely disquieting thought. What if the Ice Troll shared Ogrod's hunting methods as well as his dimensions; and there was another cunningly concealed rope-trap lying in wait for them somewhere along the trail?

The dragon and the two companions decided that in the absence of more conclusive signs, their best hope was to follow the progress of the Ice Troll, to see if it might lead them to more positive clues.

The lonely trail of footprints led them for hours along a maze of winding, diverging, branching forest routes. The troll showed no evidence of indecision, he had known exactly which twists and turns to take to reach his goal. In places he had broken off the trail again; and thrashed his way through a short cut of ripping briars and obstinate bushes of dead wood. Fortunately for the dragon, the troll had ploughed a much wider path into the undergrowth than had been absolutely necessary, perhaps a hallmark of his species' miniscule intelligence, which allowed Arangast to follow him with a minimum of stumbling, or tripping, that might upset his passengers. As for the cruelly hooked briar thorns that tried to do damage to the dragon's body as it scraped through them, the iron-tough scales snapped the sharp barbs from their stems as though they were made of straw.

At one point, two or three smaller sets of footprints converged on the Ice Troll; and a small conference seemed to have taken place. The new tracks were deemed to belong to Hobgoblins or possibly the slightly smaller Icedemons. The meeting over, the group had continued with the troll through the forest, perhaps deciding to escort the large creature on his unknown mission. From that moment on, the smell of the enemy hung thickly in the air.

Eventually the dragon and the two companions arrived at a place where the ground fell away steeply before them, sloping into a shallow valley, lying across their path. The troll's party had descended the short slope; and followed the course of the valley off to the left. The three travellers half expected to catch sight of the group tramping into the distance, as all along the meandering journey, Arangast and the two companions had had the feeling that the Winter creatures were just around the next corner; but, the Ice Troll and the goblins were nowhere to be seen.

The slopes of the valley were only sparsely populated with trees; and from their highpoint, the three travellers could follow the snowy impressions of the enemy for hundreds of paces as they followed the unusually straight course of the valley, before it finally veered to the right; and disappeared from view.

The two companions dismounted from Arangast's back, whilst he negotiated the treacherous slope. At almost every point during his descent, when he slipped or stumbled upon some snow-covered obstacle, the golden dragon cursed the Lord of Winter for his vengeful season; and it was not to be the last time the Ice Sorcerer's name was taken in vain.

Arangast safely arrived at the bottom of the slope; and Jonquil and Rattajack predictably slid down the snow bank on their backsides to join him. The terragon would have quite happily bounded back up to the top to slide down the slope again; but Jonquil, knowing this, smartly bundled him up on to the dragon's back; and the three of them started off again.

'We must be wary, my friends,' Arangast whispered, 'This place is perfect for ambush.'

'And we have no weapons,' Jonquil replied.

'Do we not?' Arangast smirked, 'I have a little hot breath at my disposal.'

Jonquil smiled to himself as he realised the folly of his words. Not all the goblin sabres or trolls axes in the world would protect the enemy from Arangast's fire. Even Jonquil, with his serious lack of worldly knowledge, knew that dragon's flame was the fiercest to be found, not even high sorcery could manufacture fire to match it.

'Well, I meant apart from your flame,' he jested.

They had only travelled a short way along the valley floor, when a fiercesome roar resounded in the distance, it was swiftly followed by a many-voiced scream of terror that seemed to echo along the walls of the valley towards them. The haunting cries were much too far away to herald an ambush; but close enough to freeze the dragon in his tracks; and strike a tone of fear amongst the two companions. They continued cautiously, suddenly attentive, searching the long ridges above them for any signs of movement.

Suddenly, a lone figure came sprinting around the bend in the valley, it was a hobgoblin, he was in the grip of blind panic, trying to run as fast as possible and look over his shoulder at the same time. He did not seem to care what lay in front of him, only the terror that pursued him from behind.

Arangast halted and began to suck in a great quantity of air, Jonquil could feel the dragon's sides swelling to accommodate the vast intake. He had the uneasy feeling, he knew what was to happen next.

Eventually, the fleeing goblin rounded the bend and turned to look ahead of him. On seeing the dragon, his face widened into an unbelieving scream of horror; and his feet slid almost ten paces before they finally brought him to a stop. He turned tail and raced back along the valley retracing his steps, then suddenly remembered the thing that had caused him to flee in the first instance and side-stepped towards the slope of the valley to attempt his escape. Arangast let forth a bolt of flame in pursuit of the creature; and a great trench seared into the snow beneath it, sending clouds of furious steam into the air. The goblin cried out as he was licked by the flame; but when the steam finally cleared, his blackened, smoking figure was seen just reaching the top of the bank and then disappeared into the forest.

'I should have killed him,' Arangast growled, 'Now he will warn his foul friends about us.'

'Then we have no time to waste,' Jonquil told him, 'We must proceed!'

Arangast agreed; and they hurried along the valley floor towards the bend. When the dragon and the two companions turned the corner, they saw that the cleft of the valley was suddenly interrupted by a rounded hillock. Apart from a few wispy saplings, struggling at its feet, the mound was devoid of trees. The hillock was crowned with a small outcrop of exposed rock; and at various other places on its gentle slopes modest clusters of jagged boulders jutted out against the otherwise smooth contours of the mound. Although finding the low hill sitting obstinately in their path, was a surprise, what really snatched the breath from their mouths was discovering a dazzling repertoire of Spring bulbs flowering in the melting snow.

The carpet of colours that were draped over the hill like a living tapestry, were as diverse as the shapes of the flowers. Bells, trumpets, starry clusters, magnificent globes; all blooming in radiant splendour. As the three approached the foot of the mound, they noticed that the thin saplings were laden with delicate blossom, the exposed ground at their roots aglow with cushions of white and yellow drops.

The travellers knew at once that this was the enchanted work of the Spring Vessel, its spell shone from the gloom of the forest like an iridescent beacon, boldly revealing its presence to the world.

Pounded into the snow at the very start of the rise, there was evidence of a great disturbance. The imprints of the troll's party were plunged into a fury of scrapings, deep gouges and confused impressions, scrambling to and fro in an aimless, riotous manner. On closer examination, the three discovered a new set of prints, much larger and heavier than the trolls; and the banf thought, strangely familiar. They beared a remarkable resemblance to the one belonging to Arangast, that Jonquil had placed his foot into by the side of the Summer pool.

The two companions dismounted from the dragon to help determine the significance of the scattered footprints. Jonquil followed a weaving set of goblin tracks to the base of a towering Longwood tree, then they mysteriously disappeared. When he looked up at the trunk, he realised why; a blackened crater had been blasted into the wood, the burn marks reaching high into the tree. Elsewhere, there were other fierce scorch marks, on trees and rocks, or huge telling bare patches on the ground, the ominous residue of a vicious struggle.

Arangast discovered an ugly pink stain of blood-soaked snow, splattered across the mêlée, surely this was where the brief confrontation had been brought to its fatal conclusion. The golden dragon examined the evidence.

'H'm!' he snorted, 'Troll's blood!'

'I wonder if it was killed,' Jonquil said looking rather nervously about him, he had visions of the maddened creature, charging from the undergrowth screaming murder with his stone hatchet.

'Dead, or soon to die,' Arangast assured him. 'One way or the other!'

Suddenly a vast shape swept over them, masking out the sinking sun for an instant; and wheeled in wide circles above their heads. Jonquil and Rattajack, instinctively dived for cover beneath Arangast's body; but the golden dragon stood his ground, unflinching, as the monstrous shadow raced across the hillock and the trees. A terrifying, winged silhouette rippled along the sunlit backcloth of the evergreen canopies, darkened the snow like a blue arrow; and stooped low at Arangast, whipping up a storm of snow particles that blustered across the three figures. The winged shape swooped low again; and turned in the air with a sudden dramatic flair to pounce like thunder on to the ground, showering the golden dragon with a blizzard of snow and leaves. Arangast stood firm, his eyes, cool and commanding.

Gorgoyle, Guardian of Spring, faced the golden dragon with equal arrogance. He was a creature of awesome majesty, his proud head crowned with a row of rising antlers, his eyes boiled with a joyful impatience, his nature sharp and volatile, like that of his creator, the Lord Fantazar. If Arangast's scales glowed with the gold of Summer, Gorgoyle's reflected the explosive power of Spring; vibrant green shades, bursting with youthful exuberance and power, his throat mirrored the radiance of the yellow flowers, shining from the extravagant covering on the hillock.

'Guardian of Summer!' he cried, Many dark days have passed since our last meeting. Do you now consort with goblins and demons?'

'Goblins and demons?' Jonquil said to himself, 'Surely he can't mean us?'

As Arangast answered, his words were tinged with the cold edge of reproach.

'Take care how you speak, Guardian of Spring. You are in the august presence of Jonquil the Wanderer and Rattajack the terragon, rescuers of the Sacred Vessel of Summer.'

Gorgoyle peered beneath Arangast's legs at the two, sheltering companions, he seemed little impressed.

'They smell of the enemy to me,' he sniffed.

'Then your senses tell you lies, Gorgoyle!' Arangast snapped.

The green dragon strolled loftily around Arangast's tensed body, the Summer dragon had not been prepared for such a hostile greeting. Perhaps, the hot blood of battle had not had time to cool in Gorgoyle's veins. As the haughty Spring dragon passed by Jonquil and Rattajack, he threw them a few distinctly unfriendly glances, that made a shiver crawl across the banf's skin. Then he returned to face Arangast.

'You say these two creatures rescued the Summer Vessel?' he said.

'That is true,' Arangast answered through tight lips.

'Are they also responsible for tying it up like a piece of common baggage?' Gorgoyle continued.

'How else was I meant to carry it? In my teeth?' Arangast replied.

'Who gave you the authority to move the Summer Vessel? Our orders were only to seek and find!',Gorgoyle questioned him.

Arangast decided to change the direction of the argument slightly.

'The Winter servants you just despatched, Gorgoyle, did you recognise them?'

'Certainly not!' the Spring dragon retorted, 'They were just filthy trolls and goblins.'

'I'll wager they were the same troll and goblins that buried the Spring Vessel on the mound a few days ago,' Arangast told him.

'But why would they return? For what purpose?' Gorgoyle asked.

Gorgoyle, Guardian of Spring faced the golden dragon.

'To destroy, Gorgoyle, to destroy!' Arangast growled, 'Look at the hill, see what the magic of the Vessel has done to it! The enemy thought the Sacred Vessels were powerless without the crystals; but they were wrong, the precious boxes have enchantment of their own; and they have used it to thwart the evil one's plans. Now the enemy have discovered this, they are returning to claim the Vessels a second time, to destroy them! We have to rescue the Vessels and restore them to our masters before all is lost. That is why we have been searching for you. To help you!'

'To help me!' Gorgoyle cried, 'Arangast, you speak of decisions that are not yours to make. I do not need your help. I shall remain here and defend the Spring Vessel against all attackers!'

'Then through your folly, Gorgoyle,' Arangast began, 'Both you and the Spring Vessel shall be destroyed; and the fate of the world sealed forever.'

Jonquil could see that Arangast's argument was having no effect on the intransigent Spring dragon; and he could keep his silence no longer. He leaped out from beneath Arangast's body and boldly addressed the stubborn Gorgoyle.

'Arangast is right!' he exclaimed, 'The enemy is upon us. Winter has taken over the forest. We are not safe!'

Gorgoyle eyed the banf thoroughly and then a sneer broke across his face.

'So,' he began, 'The goblin can talk!'

Jonquil stood his ground and stared the dragon bravely in the eye.

'If you please, Sir,' he said, 'I am not a goblin, I am a banf. A member of an ancient and most noble race of forest dwellers; and you, Sir, are discourteous!'

The Spring dragon's eyes narrowed in contempt at this unexpected display of bravado by the banf; and his head suddenly drew backwards to its fullest height. For a few terrible moments, Jonquil was confident the dragon was going to roast him, he could hear a deep rumble growing in Arangast's throat; and he thought he heard the Summer dragon growl, 'Gorgoyle . . . if you dare!' Suddenly, Rattajack sprang forward through Arangast's legs and reared up to shield Jonquil's body. He snarled at Gorgoyle and spat two sparks which hissed angrily into the snow at the Spring dragon's feet. The great beast was so amazed at the terragon's fiery advance that he took a step in retreat from his small adversary.

The terragon fixed the dumbfounded dragon with his sparkling, amber gaze. Gorgoyle's eyes widened in wonder, his jaws opened as if to speak but no sound emerged, his face took on a catalogue of expressions; surprise, incredulity, anger, amusement, remorse. The only movement from Rattajack was the occasional, involuntary flicker of his ears; his eyes never left their target.

Gradually Gorgoyle's demeanour softened; and he bowed to Jonquil.

'Jonquil the banf, I have to apologise. Please forgive my arrogant folly.'

A totally speechless Jonquil returned the bow. Arangast laughed aloud.

'Rattajack! The silent diplomat!' he said, 'Why didn't I think of it?'

Gorgoyle turned at last to Arangast.

'Well, brother Guardian,' he began, 'It seems there is great adventure afoot. With the help of our two friends, I shall raise the Spring Vessel from its shallow grave, then let us away, to find Snarlgard and the Sacred Vessel of Autumn.'

Flight to Danger

Jonquil and Rattajack helped Gorgoyle raise the Sacred Spring Vessel from the mound, then the fabulous article was strapped securely to the Spring dragon's back. Jonquil could only gasp in wonder when he saw that the Spring Vessel matched the Summer Vessel, gold for gold, jewel for jewel; and a dazzling portrait of Gorgoyle graced the underside of the former's lid as one of Arangast did the latter's.

Gorgoyle insisted that Jonquil climb up with the chest on his back; and allow him to carry the banf on their journey. So, the two companions, now having a dragon each to ride; they all set off from the colourful hillock.

Tiny crystals of ice clustered on the petals of a delicate White Drop, the edges of its leaves began to curl and wither; the sap slowly froze within its fragile stem. The flower's head bowed in concession and it was dead.

The dragon's procession had not gone far from the hillock, when Jonquil asked Gorgoyle a question that had been burning in his mind for quite some time.

'What happened to the large troll that returned to the mound?' he began, 'We saw the blood from the fight; but we never actually found out what really happened to him. Did he escape?'

Gorgoyle turned to look full into the banf's eyes; and a strange menacing smile flickered across his face, Jonquil suddenly felt a little uncomfortable.

'Would you like me to show you his remains?' the dragon offered.

Jonquil gulped.

'Er . . . n'no!' he stammered, 'That won't be necessary!'

The procession continued for quite a while in thoughtful silence.

To Arangast's dismay, there were no new tracks to be seen; and the light was now failing fast. Gorgoyle suggested they find a suitable place to rest for the night; and resume their search in the morning, lest they should miss some vital clue in the increasing gloom; but Arangast disagreed.

'No!' he cried. 'Tomorrow will be too late! Snarlgard is in great danger, we must find him tonight!'

'But how, Arangast?' Gorgoyle asked him, 'We have no trail to follow.'

The Summer Guardian answered the Spring Guardian with a calm smile.

'Have no fear, Gorgoyle, I have a plan.'

Arangast turned to the banf, 'Jonquil, I have need of you in this, will you help me?'

The banf leapt from Gorgoyle's back and without hesitation said he would. Then the Summer dragon informed him that it would mean him being separated from Rattajack for a time, whilst he accompanied Arangast on a dangerous errand. Suddenly Jonquil was not quite so sure; Rattajack had always been at his side, the two of them had never been apart. The banf was not sure if he would be able to stand leaving the terragon behind. Rattajack trotted up to him and looked deeply into his eyes; the two powerful amber orbs seemed to calm his fears; and somehow Jonquil knew that it would be all right. He turned back to Arangast and reaffirmed his consent.

'Where are we going?' he asked out of interest.

'Up there,' Arangast replied; and he raised his eyes to the roof of the forest.

'Y'You mean f'flying,' Jonquil stammered, 'I'In the air?'

'Of course,' the dragon answered him. 'Gorgoyle, you must remain here with Rattajack to protect the Sacred Vessels. Try to conceal yourselves in the undergrowth and keep safe. If we have not returned by morning, it will surely mean that Snarlgard is dead, the Autumn Vessel destroyed; and that we ourselves have fallen. You must then decide for yourselves which road you will take! Jonquil, untie the Summer Vessel from my back and use the treevines to make yourself a harness. Quickly, my friend, every moment is precious!'

Jonquil rushed over to Rattajack and hugged him, long and hard, the terragon let a tiny whimper escape whilst he was wrapped in the banf's arms. Arangast hurried Jonquil.

'We must make haste!'

Jonquil gave the terragon's head a final pat and then climbed aboard the Summer dragon. He made sure Arangast waited until he had securely tied himself on and tested the strength of his knots a good many times. Then the Summer dragon made his move.

The two great flaps of leathery skin, that were Arangast's wings, unravelled themselves either side of the securely strapped banf. The dragon raised them high over his back; and Jonquil had the strangest feeling he was sitting inside a narrow tent. All the banf could see was the long, sweeping neck and noble head of the Summer dragon. Arangast took one last look at the two who were staying behind; and then dropped down low. With a great surge of strength, the dragon thrust himself upwards, beating down hard with his wings. The banf was thrown backwards and forwards along the dragon's spine, his stomach heaving like a pendulum, as Arangast attacked the air. As strong as the dragon was, the ascending flight through the trees was rough and scrappy. In places, the branches formed a criss-cross barrier between the trunks; and Arangast had to force his way through them, using his powerful antlers to wrench the dead wood aside, with forceful, bough-breaking sweeps.

By the time they had cleared the roof of the forest, Jonquil's back was thoroughly branch beaten and bruised. There were small twigs decorating his pigtails and surprisingly one or two leaf husks had found their way into his mouth, which he promptly spat out.

Rattajack watched the dark shape of the dragon grow smaller and smaller, until it finally drifted out of sight. The terragon turned mournfully to Gorgoyle. The Spring dragon tried to offer words of comfort but there was nothing he could say.

Rattajack helped him drag the Sacred Vessels into the dense bushes, then Gorgoyle curled his long body around them, draping his dull, leathery wing over their brilliant surfaces. The terragon carefully climbed inside the dragon's coils and settled down for the night, both of them resting as silent as the grave to wait for morning.

Jonquil and Arangast were quite some distance above the tops of the trees, the dragon circling ever upwards with slow, rhythmic beats. The banf suddenly felt an almost unbearable pressure in his large ears, instinctively he swallowed, there was a loud pop and they were clear. The constant breeze rippled through his hair and clothes; and misted his eyes at first, so that he could not see. Eventually, they cleared and Jonquil caught his first ever glimpse of the world beyond the forest. In the distance, the Western edge of the Green Sky, darkened to a saw-toothed silhouette standing against a fading, ruby inferno; above them, the moon and stars were already bright in the sky.

Jonquil had often dreamed about what it would be like to finally step out from the forest and gaze upon the outside world; but none of the mental pictures he had drawn came even close to the glorious reality; it was so big; so wide; and so open. Not a single tree to mar his view, no network of tangled branches to obscure the sky.

Jonquil looked down at the gently rotating panorama; the trees looked so closely packed together, it seemed impossible that anything could live beneath them.

'Gorgoyle and Rattajack are down there somewhere,' Jonquil thought to himself. 'How will Arangast ever find his way back? It all looks the same, like a dense, living carpet. Where are the distinguishing features to guide our return? Where are the landmarks?'

'You are very quiet back there,' Arangast cried, 'has the wind got your tongue?' Arangast's head swivelled round to look back at his seated passenger.

'It's wonderful!' Jonquil shouted.

'Have you got over your nerves yet?' the dragon asked.

'Er . . . yes! of course!' Jonquil lied.

In spite of himself, the banf was beginning to enjoy this head-spinning experience. He had always known that the Green Sky Forest was big; but now he could see just how vast it really was; the sea of trees stretched before them in all directions, as far as the eye could see. In places the great forest rose and fell in shallow waves, as it flowed over hills and down into valleys; occasional white outcrops ruptured its textured surface, minor snow-clad mountains, standing head and shoulders above the arboreal millions.

'I cannot believe this is happening!' Jonquil shouted to Arangast, 'It's wonderful!'

'Good,' said Arangast, 'but now we must set our minds to more serious matters. Keep your eyes on the forest and tell me the instant you see anything.'

'But what are we looking for?' Jonquil cried, desperately battling to make himself heard over the roaring wind, that seemed to get louder the higher they climbed.

'Fire!' Arangast replied. 'Dragon's fire! Now that it is almost dark, Snarlgard's flame will shine like a beacon.'

'Is this part of your plan?' the banf shouted.

'No, Jonquil, this *is* my plan, for what it is worth! What we shall do when we find the Guardian of Autumn, *if* we find him, I have not yet decided. I only pray that we are not too late!'

The dragon climbed a little higher; and then stretched out his wings to harness the energy of the wind in a full glide. He dropped his right wing and wheeled into a wide circle, although this meant Jonquil was now tipped at a rather unsettling angle, at least he could see more of the forest below.

The tops of the trees were becoming increasingly difficult to identify in the creeping darkness; the tall, evergreen Longwoods, speared through the canopy like dark guards, marching in fragmented armies; the broad, light-stealing Green Oaks, spotted the forest like extravagant rosettes; the Iron Beech, the Silver Plane, the Paper Birch; all jostled with each other for the affection of the sun; but in the descending cloak of darkness, they were simply closely-knit pieces in a revolving patchwork blanket of greys and deep blues, rapidly fading into a swamp of gloom.

Arangast took them a little lower, his gliding gradually gaining speed. The steady rush of frosty air that streamed over the dragon's body, bit sharply into Jonquil's cheeks, causing fresh wells of water to seep into his eyes; and the banf's tightly gripped fingers started to grow numb on the reins. The dragon was growing impatient; he started to compliment his swift progress with agitated wing bursts. The freezing wind tugged at the banf's shoulders, trying to dislodge him from his seat, he was grasping the treevine reins so tightly, the whites of his knuckles shone through his skin. Jonquil decided it was not very wise to place so much faith in his ability to tie knots, so he leaned forward as far as he could until he was lying as flat as possible along the dragon's spine; the wind roaring in his ears and whipping through his hair.

'I hope this dragon remembers he has got a passenger!' the banf muttered to himself.

Arangast craned his neck frantically back and forth, in an effort to scan the world below; at times his head disappeared right underneath his body, lest he should miss any vital signs of his comrade. Jonquil was too busy holding on for dear life to be of any use to him now; and when the dragon shouted back to him, could he see anything, he quite truthfully answered, 'No!' What he did not tell the dragon was that his head was buried firmly between his fists, eyes tightly closed. Eventually, the dragon slowed his frenzied pace and returned to a more relaxed, planing flight. Jonquil was able to sit up a little and wipe the streaming tears from his eyes.

When the mist cleared he saw that evening had advanced to night, the forest had disappeared; and in its place was an endless black ocean. The sky was now the deepest, inky blue and set in its ceiling were countless clusters of shimmering diamante; the snow clouds, that had threatened violent repetitions of the first downpour, had retreated unfulfilled beyond the horizon; leaving the world naked to the biting frost.

'Where are you, Snarlgard?' Arangast called despairingly to the wind.

'What can have happened to him?' Jonquil asked.

'He must be dead! Killed by the enemy! If he was alive, we would see his fire,' the dragon cried.

'Perhaps the enemy haven't found him yet,' Jonquil offered.

'No!' Arangast shouted back, 'that is not possible! The forest is crawling with the Ice Sorcerer's servants, they are sure to have found him.'

The banf could see that the dragon was rapidly losing heart, he was determined that Arangast would not give up, and concede to failure.

'But he could be anywhere! The forest is a big place and the trees grow so thickly. Perhaps we are too high to see his flames. Fly lower, fly lower!' The banf urged him.

Arangast swiftly complied; and without word of warning, closed half of his wingspan, suddenly diving into a plummeting spiral. The shock of this violent drop forced a cry of sheer horror from Jonquil's lips, the black mass of the forest filled his vision, the dragon's head pointing uncompromisingly, straight at it. The speed of Arangast's descent caused a hurricane of wind to beat against the banf's body, hurling him backwards, his treevine harnesses squealed with the effort of holding him in place. Jonquil had awful premonitions of the vines snapping under the strain of the wind's demands; and his helpless body being wrenched off into space, without the great dragon even knowing. Arangast was showing no signs of slowing their fall or levelling out over the forest; and for one terrible moment it looked as though the dragon meant to kill them both, in a spinning suicide dive.

Suddenly, Jonquil's eyes were distracted by a flash in the forest, off to their left side; he shouted with all his might so that Arangast would hear him above the howling wind; and the dragon's wings swept out like two, billowing sails to catch the air; and with a mighty swoop they screamed over the forest canopy, skimming the very tips of the tallest trees.

'Did you see something?' Arangast called to the banf.

The dragon's violent aerobatics had left Jonquil feeling decidedly ill, he was sure that if it was daylight his face would look a most unhealthy shade of green. The banf needed a few, deep breaths and a moment's composure, before he could finally bring himself to answer.

'The flame!' he thought he shouted but it emerged as a weak mumble.

'What?' Arangast cried, 'I cannot hear you!'

Jonquil seized his head in his hands to try and stop it swimming and said again, 'The flame!'

'You saw it!' the dragon exclaimed.

'Over to the left,' the banf told him.

Arangast turned his head around to look at Jonquil, his eyes were wide with excitement.

'Show me!' he said.

Jonquil pointed in the vague direction he had seen the fire; and as he did so, another bright pool of light flickered beneath the trees.

'Snarlgard!' the dragon cried 'It has to be.'

'What are we going to do now?' Jonquil asked.

'We are going in of course.'

'But . . .' Jonquil began.

'Hold on my friend!' Arangast cried.

The dragon raced towards the spot where they had seen the flame, roaring over the tree tops, stirring their branches with his draught. When they reached the place, Arangast wheeled above it in slow, reconnoitring circles, both he and the banf staring down through the unusually leafy branches of a gargantuan Green Oak into the eye of a raging storm of battle.

Below them the forest floor was alive with moving figures; softly filtered shafts of moonlight picked out armoured bodies, stark against the white ground; but it was the ferocious blasts of dragon fire that fully illuminated the scene and revealed the true nature of the assault.

Somewhere within the rising cacophony of battle cries was the fiercesome roar of Snarlgard; as Arangast circled the mêlée, the Autumn dragon came into view. He was pinned up against the great trunk of the Green Oak, his body half concealing a small cavity formed by the twisted roots, in which, undoubtedly the Sacred Vessel of Autumn had been hidden. The Guardian was besieged by a chanting mob of Winter creatures, two or three hundred strong; who were attacking him in small, ankle-nipping parties, testing his strength, draining his energy. The creatures seemed surprisingly well organised and disciplined; and were bating the Autumn dragon with cunning and restraint, rather than just charging him as a mad, screaming horde. The attack was only being conducted, however, on one side of the tree, when it would have made good battle sense, from the enemy's point of view, to surround the dragon completely; and draw his fire from every angle at once, eventually driving him to exhaustion. Although the creatures were only using this technique to half of its effectiveness, by the growing sluggish response of the dragon, it was clearly beginning to take its toll.

Arangast turned to Jonquil.

'The Autumn Guardian is tiring,' he began, 'We do not have much time. This is what I propose we do.'

Arangast then proceeded to tell Jonquil the details of his hastily devised plan and what he wanted the banf to do; Jonquil felt his heart leap into his mouth as he listened to the dragon's words, never had he missed the comforting presence of Rattajack more or the warmth and safety of his banf home so far away.

Arangast told him that he was going to hover as close to the canopy of the Green Oak as he could manage, then the banf was to jump from the dragon's back into the uppermost branches of the tree and stay there until the battle beneath was over and it was safe to descend. Arangast would then try to find a suitable place to land, behind the enemy lines; and attack them from the rear. He explained to Jonquil that he dared not leave the banf alone on the ground, for the trails of the forest were clearly bristling with goblins and trolls; and the prospect of the banf's capture or execution by the enemy was unthinkable. Jonquil felt like telling Arangast that the prospect of him missing his grip on a Green Oak branch, falling to earth and breaking his neck was equally unthinkable; but decided against it. Arangast was simply trying to make the best of an impossible situation; and the tree seemed to be the lesser of the two evils. Jonquil began to loosen his bonds in readiness for his 'great leap for banfkind'; to his horror he found that the knots of his harness came undone with sickening ease, the dragon's wild flying antics had clearly strained them to within a hair's breadth of pulling free and relinquishing him to the wind.

The dragon slowly descended on the Green Oak, the banf carefully rose to his feet and clasping Arangast's snaked back neck, balanced himself for the jump. The strangely dense foliage of the tree made it difficult for Jonquil to pick his landing, the occasional bright bursts of dragon-fire from below allowed him to see one or two thick branches to aim for; but the margin for error was frighteningly small. Arangast hovered as low as he dared, without fear of stalling or becoming tangled in the tree tops, the dreaded moment arrived and he shouted the word to Jonquil; after taking the deepest breath of his life, the banf launched himself into the air. The dragon turned away as his small friend fell into the darkness; and he prayed he had done the right thing as he heard Jonquil crashing through the upper branches.

Arangast sped on over the trees, searching for a good landing place. Eventually, he approached a small clearing, some distance behind the advancing lines of the enemy; after he had lowered himself into a safe descent; and made sure there were no witnesses to his arrival, to deny him the element of surprise. He bade the articulate, intelligent creature into which the Summer Wizard's sorcery had transformed him, step aside; and allow the former ferocious monster, that once had raged in the bowels of the Throne Citadel to return and bring forth the fires of hell, to do battle with the enemy. Arangast felt a deep, thunderous roar beginning to grow within his soul, a roar fuelled by the anger and revulsion he had borne at the Ice Sorcerer's desecration of the hallowed Vessels; but he would save it, restrain it, until the moment when he stood before the ranks of the evil servants and was able to belch forth his flowing river of wrath.

Now Jonquil knew what an Autumn leaf felt like hanging by its last thread, waiting only for the sharp tug of the breeze to whisk it into the air and float it gently to the ground. Although he doubted if *his* descent to the forest floor would be quite so graceful.

The banf was dangling, precariously from the broken end of a stout branch that jutted out a short distance from the trunk of the Green Oak. The jagged end had hooked itself under the folds of his shoulder-cloak, after he had crashed into it on his downwards journey from the canopy. Jonquil had been bounced from branch to bough, after his rude arrival in the tree. He had tried to grasp a hundred limbs as they had appeared before him; but they either threw him aside or snapped free in his hands, eventually, the broken bough had brought him to a jarring halt; almost throttling him in the process. Showers of leaves and twigs had accompanied him on his battered descent, most of which now protruded from his hair and clothes, the remainder had rained down on the raging dragon below.

Jonquil was suspended, like a sad marionette, about halfway down the tree; gazing between his dangling feet, he was able to enjoy, if that is the word, a bird's eye view of the battle on the ground. Snarlgard was fighting bravely, spraying the massed attackers with great sheets of flame, he was also using his strong muscular tail as a monstrous whip, thrashing the charging tribes, sending them rolling back, maimed and broken along the ground; but the clans of the dark servants were gathering in force, more and more columns seemed to be marching in to join their brethren from the surrounding forest, the Autumn Guardian was hopelessly outnumbered.

The Winter creatures knew that they only needed to destroy one Sacred Vessel to ensure the downfall of the Wizards of Light; and they had clearly decided that Snarlgard's Vessel was to be the chosen one; and they were determined to make sure, by sheer presence of numbers, that they did not fail this time.

From his lofty vantage point, Jonquil discovered why the enemy were only engaging Snarlgard on one side of the tree, growing healthily on the other side were two large House Mushrooms, the sight of the familiar fungi tugged mercilessly at his heart. The dark creatures were clearly unwilling to approach the mushrooms; and were resigned to fighting the battle, giving the two fungi a decidedly wide berth. The banf wished there was some way in which he could aid Snarlgard in his hour of need; but his orders were to remain in the tree (though not necessarily in such an uncomfortable position as his present one) until Arangast arrived on the scene and the battle was done. Although, by the rate the armies of the Ice Sorcerer were marching in to reinforce their side, the banf was beginning to wonder whether the Summer Guardian and Snarlgard together would be enough to defeat them.

Jonquil tentatively reached upwards until he found the jagged end of the branch that had seized his cloak. He had to be very careful, the gaps between the branches below him were a lot wider; and if he should fall, there would be nothing to save him from hurtling all the way to the ground. He did not relish the thought of introducing himself to the Autumn dragon by dropping violently into his lap. He grasped the end of the branch and slowly rotated himself until he was facing the trunk, the material had now drawn even tighter around his throat. He then swung his legs upwards and wrapped them securely around the branch, the banf finally managed to wrench his cloak free of the jagged fibres and began to crawl feet first towards the trunk, suspended beneath the stout limb.

Suddenly, the evil armies below launched a fierce attack on the beleaguered dragon, swarming upon him in their first real show of strength, Snarlgard answered them with a blistering torrent of fire, that for a few moments seemed to light up the entire forest. Jonquil felt a wave of heat wash over him from below; and suddenly the whole of the tree above was illuminated as bright as day. The boughs of the Green Oak were thickly furnished with luxuriant foliage, the leaves shining back at the banf with the radiance of polished copper and bronze; rich tints of gold, ruby and topaz studded the roof of the tree's canopy. The enchantment from the Autumn Vessel, stashed inside the twisted roots of the Green Oak, had seeped from its wooden casket and been drawn up through the veins of the tree to create an explosion of rich colours in an otherwise naked forest. Jonquil imagined that in daylight the Green Oak would shine out like a standard bearer, announcing to all the whereabouts of its prize.

Snarlgard, Guardian of Autumn answered them with a blistering torrent of fire.

Jonquil had almost reached the gnarled trunk, when an ominous crack sounded before him, he tried to hurry himself along the branch but then another loud report followed the first. With each nerve-jarring sound, the banf felt the branch sink a little lower until with a protesting squeal it finally conceded to his weight and swung downwards. Luckily for Jonquil Green Oaks were made of tough, sinewy fibres and the bough did not break cleanly, rather than snapping free and abandoning him to the air, it pulled him sharply in towards the trunk. Jonquil met the hard, deeply grooved bark with a solid thump. His legs thrashed frantically at the tree trying to find a hold, the branch finally gave in to his squirming weight and ripped loose from the trunk, at the very last moment Jonquil's grasping right hand found a strong treevine and he was slammed against the bark once again.

By the time the swirling spots and stars cleared from his eyes, Jonquil had decided that a leaf's life was not for him, he was far safer on the ground, beneath the House Mushrooms. Using the trunk-hugging vines as a conveniently grown rope ladder, the banf negotiated his descent. At one point, however, to his dismay, he discovered that the treevines were only growing on the battle side of the Green Oak, which effectively dashed his hopes of sneaking quietly down the mushroom side of the tree to reach his enchanted shelter. If he was to continue his present course of descent he would probably end up sitting on Snarlgard's head. Jonquil inspected the vineless path down the tree, the bark of the Green Oak was a mass of gnarled growths and callouses, which he decided should make easy climbing. What the banf could not see from above, was a glistening ice patch, half melted on the trunk formed by a volley of ice-javelins hurled, rather inaccurately, by the Icedemons, at the dragon. The heat from Snarlgard's fire had caused them to thaw on the bark and now they had formed a long slippery coat across the banf's intended path.

Jonquil was just about to pride himself on his nimble progress, when his feet suddenly shot from beneath him, the speed of his slip giving him no chance to reach for a firm hold. In a strange kind of bear-hug the banf rapidly slid down the trunk, his leggings and tunic becoming soaked by the melting ice. The more Jonquil tried to grip the smooth, wet surface, the faster he slipped; his fingers stang with the cold but he forced them to dig deep into the ice to try and slow his fall; but to no avail. He was just about to console himself that at least he would have a relatively soft landing amongst the House Mushrooms growing beneath him, when he struck a particularly bulbous, gnarled growth protruding from the twisted bark, about a third of the way up the tree, which launched the banf at a most undesirable angle, landing him right in the middle of the battle ground.

Jonquil lay as still as possible on the damp ground, the enemy must surely have seen him, he had fallen directly between them and the dragon; and this time he had not forgotten about the magic of the Fallon leaves, as he had been thrown forcefully out from the tree, he noticed, to his horror, that all of the enchanted leaves had been stripped from his legs by the violence of his descent. Now he was truly alone and defenceless. The only thing he could think of was to play dead and hope for the best. The Winter creatures seemed to be holding a war council and the various tribes of Hobgoblins, Ice Trolls and Icedemons were gathered around their two leaders, to discuss the final plan for the dragon's destruction. They were all huddled together in tight groups and to the banf's great relief had been too deeply engrossed in their tactical plots to notice his fall from the tree.

Jonquil was lying facing the dragon and the Green Oak, he gazed longingly at the two House Mushrooms and speculated on his chances of making them alive, if he were to try a mad dash for it. Then he remembered the Icedemons and their deadly javelins, he certainly did not relish the thought of staggering beneath the rim of the nearest mushroom with a spear of ice impaled between his shoulder blades. Then the sickening smell of burning flesh drifted to his nostrils; and he very carefully turned his head to look around him.

Jonquil's stomach turned as his eyes fell on the broken, scorched remains of a hobgoblin, lying uncomfortably close to him. The smoke was still rising from its blackened, shrivelled body into the cold air. The creature's face was contorted into a frozen expression of sheer hate mixed with terrible pain; its jaws were fully gaped; and the fragmented shards of moonlight were reflected in its cruel fangs and rows of sharpened, flesh-tearing teeth. In places, great portions of its skin had been seared from its bones by the deadly lick of the dragon's flame, the distinctive long plumes of hair that the goblins wore as shaggy manes had been razed to a balded, smoking stubble; tiny embers still lifting into the breeze. The only part of the goblin that had not been severely affected by the fire was its armour; and suddenly an idea leapt into Jonquil's mind.

The creature's helmet had fallen just within the banf's reach and at a snail's pace his hand moved towards it, his movements would have been barely discernible by someone standing over him in broad daylight; but in the heavy darkness beneath the canopies; and with the absence of dragon fire, the banf looked like just another corpse as he slowly drew the helmet towards him. Jonquil discovered that the metal was still warm; and when he finally gathered enough courage to reach for the armour on the body he found that to be quite hot. To the banf's disgust, to obtain all the necessary pieces of the protective covering he needed, he was required to touch the charred corpse to free the breast plate from beneath it. The banf crept as smoothly as he could towards the dead goblin, until they were literally lying side by side, his fingers unintentionally broke through the creature's brittle, calcined rib-cage as he tried to push the body on to its side to free the metal piece. Jonquil's skin crawled in protest as the goblin's damp, tepid interior closed around his intruding fingers. At last the breast plate pulled free and the banf was able to adorn himself with his goblin disguise. It was no easy job, applying the dead creature's armour whilst remaining perfectly flat to the ground; and Jonquil only daring to move his hands painfully slowly; one way or another he managed it.

Suddenly a great cry went up behind him, a chorus of foul voices that rang through the trees with harsh notes and discord, deep booming sounds followed, that seemed to pound a crude rhythm. The creatures had found hollow logs and were beating them with their clubs and swords, the strangled cacophony that writhed through the air was intended to be singing, or the nearest noise the monsters and gargoyles could manage. As they screeched, hundreds of assorted feet stamped in time on the slushy ground.

The enemy officers had concluded their tactical consultations with the mob and were now leading their hordes in an evil chant of destruction. The tortured melody grew in volume as it filtered through the ranks of creatures until all of the collected armies added their screaming voices to the hellish choir. Eventually the unintelligible verses ceased, when one of the two leaders jumped on to a prominent tree stump and held his jewelled club aloft for silence. It was Hobba, the prince of Hobgoblins, his brother had mingled through the crowds urging them to sing the chant; but now all were quiet. The goblin twin growled a few insistent orders at his minions, in their own ugly language; and then the howling chant began again; this time in the tongue of the wizards, so that Snarlgard could hear and understand the true menace of their words.

Jonquil shivered with fear as the murderous voices drifted over him towards the dragon; and he dared not imagine what plans the creatures had in store to follow their vile chant.

Snarlgard wearily lifted his head to stare with contempt into the sea of sneering, hating faces that spat their evil verses at him.

Hobba thumped his heel on the platform of wood, to keep the beat, conducting his gruesome orchestra into the words of the chant.

'Kill the dragon — chop him up!
Tear his throat out — chop him up!
Gouge his eyes out — chop him up!
Break his bones — chop him up!
DESTROY! DESTROY! DESTROY!
Stab his heart — chop him up!
Chop his head off — chop him up!
Spill his blood — chop him up!
Grind his teeth — chop him up!
DESTROY! DESTROY! DESTROY!
Find his Vessel — chop it up!
Smash its jewels — chop it up!
Steal its gold — chop it up!
Break its power — chop it up!
DESTROY! DESTROY! DESTROY!'

The chant continued in the same vein for a good many more verses, promising death or violation to all the noble peoples of Enchantica. When the screeching hordes began to hurl insults at the Wizards of Light, specifically the Lord Waxifrade; Snarlgard could contain his fury no longer.

The dragon leapt to his feet, charged forward and blasted a stream of white hot fire at Hobba. The goblin prince, who had thought that his tree-stump was out of the dragon's reach, was taken completely off guard by Snarlgard's surging advance; his eyes exploded in terror as he saw the dragon's jaws open before him; and his smug, arrogant voice rose to a piercing scream, as the white fire blew him from his perch and shrivelled him mid-air.

The snow hissed angrily as Hobba's smouldering corpse fell to the ground.

The dragon hurried back to his place of guard by the tree and a cry of horror and dismay rose from the crowds, a group of them converged on the swirling plumes of smoke and steam rising from the blackened figure in the snow.

Bledderag suddenly leapt on to the tree-stump, brandishing both his and Hobba's jewelled battle clubs; he screamed the attack and the whole of the gathered hordes, incensed at the dragon's outrage, turned and charged at the Green Oak.

Jonquil lay frozen, his face thrust downwards into the slush, listening to the pounding feet of the enemy rushing past him, splattering showers of mud and leaves over his quickly donned helmet. The banf felt the ground shake every time one of the heavy Ice Trolls thundered by and prayed that they had the consideration not to step on him, or that would surely mean an end to it. He waited until he was certain all of the dark creatures had surged past him and engaged the dragon, then he sprang to his feet, ready to creep around the outside of the conflict and dive under the safety of the mushrooms; but what he saw before him, filled him with shame for thinking only of his own safety. Snarlgard was swamped with stabbing, thrusting, slashing bodies, the great Ice Trolls were wading through the writhing figures of their faster goblin brethren, to get a good swing at the dragon's besieged body with their mighty stone axes. Scores of the smaller creatures tore at Snarlgard's thrashing wings; ripping gaping tears into the leathery skin; a forest of spears thrust at his face, cruel points meaning to blind him. Storms of rocks, knives and ice-javelins rained down on his scarred flanks, crashing and bruising his steely scales; but still the dragon fought on.

Snarlgard's powerful tail wrenched the smothering ranks asunder, sweeping the legs from under the front line attackers, condemning them to be crushed by their own fellows pushing from behind; but for every ten creatures he despatched, another twenty lunged forward to take their place.

Where was Arangast? He should have made it to the battle by now? Without him Snarlgard was surely doomed. Jonquil stood helplessly watching the imminent slaughter of the Guardian of Autumn, knowing that he could not simply stand by and do nothing to help the dragon. Firmly grasped in the dead goblin's hand was a battle club, Jonquil bent down and snatched it from the creature's grip, as he did so, he was rammed violently from behind. An Icedemon late for the battle; but anxious not to miss out on the killing had been running with his shield held up high to his face, consequently he had not seen the banf's doubled over form and crashed into him. Jonquil leapt to his feet to face the creature, the demon, who was roughly the same size as the banf, climbed to his feet cursing him in some foul, grating language, shook his fists at Jonquil and then trotted past him to join in with the rest. The demon had clearly thought the banf to be a goblin and his disguise had been helped by standing with his back to the dragon's fire, so the demon could only see Jonquil in silhouette.

The banf had all the proof he needed and he turned to give chase to the stumbling Icedemon, with a hefty swipe, he knocked the creature's helmet off; and then swiftly followed with a full crack on the back of its head. He had felled his first

The Icedemon shook his fist at Jonquil.

enemy soldier. The Icedemon was to be the first of many, the banf began by keeping to the fringes of the mob, picking off any individuals that were foolish enough to stray from the main groups. The small collection of goblins and demons that the banf coshed, after cheekily lifting off their helmets first, literally never knew what hit them; and before he knew what he'd done, Jonquil had removed at least a dozen enemy creatures from active service.

A little way ahead of him, in the midst of the violent scrummage, was a large Ice Troll, pelting the dragon with rocks, supplied from a bulging sack hanging from his belt. The monster was Bolg; one of the Vessel thieves; in fact, the very troll that lifted the Autumn Vessel; and somehow Snarlgard knew it. Despite the fact that the dragon was being attacked by more screaming devils than he could count, like a caterpillar furiously set upon by army ants, he was determined to get to the troll; but whenever Snarlgard tried to blast the tall creature, Bolg kept him pinned down with a volley of missiles. The troll was laughing aloud at the dragon like a gigantic gormless child having suddenly discovered an entertaining new game. Jonquil decided that the time had come for Bolg to pay for his fun.

Completely forgetting about the danger to himself, the banf elbowed and barged his way through the jostling ranks of the enemy, he poked at least two individuals in the eye, stamped on countless creatures' toes; and at one point dug his hands under the armpits of a slightly shorter Icedemon and physically heaved him into the air and threw him aside. Jonquil raged his way through the mob, he simply had to reach the large troll; what had started out as the lumbering oaf's mindless game, was now becoming a serious threat to Snarlgard's life and the banf was the only one who could stop him. The Autumn dragon was so preoccupied with dodging and fending off the hurtling rocks, that he had stopped breathing fire, this enabled the front line of goblins and demons to surge forward and grapple with the great beast; some even daring the climb on to his back to stab at his scales with their cruel spears.

Jonquil eventually wrestled his way to the troll, the top of the banf's helmet barely reached the monster's waistband, so knocking him unconscious was clearly out of the question, the banf decided to concentrate on Bolg's arsenal, the sack of rocks. The crowd of pushing bodies around Jonquil swayed and flowed like a river and he found it a major task to keep his position behind the troll. As a stream of charging goblins barged past him, the banf's hand accidentally caught on the hilt of a sword, lying in its sheath on one of their belts; his fingers instinctively closed around it; and as the goblin moved forward, the blade was slowly drawn from its home. The bottom of the troll's rock sack was almost dragging in the slush from the weight; and Jonquil had to drop down to his hands and knees to stab at it. The tough material had been drawn as tight as a drum by the heavy stones and at first was most reluctant to yield to the goblin blade; but luckily all the enemy creatures had been ordered to sharpen their weapons by The Twins, in readiness for the battle with the dragon; and as soon as the cutting edge of the sword took hold, the fibres sprang away from it, causing a small hole to appear. The sheer weight of the sack's cargo did the rest and a torrent of hefty boulders escaped from the growing vent. The banf thought the least he could do was inform the lofty creature of his loss, so he pushed the spilling sack into the troll's body; and then Bolg's exposed toes received the direct attention of a dozen evacuating rocks.

The Ice Troll screamed like a slapped baby when the pain from his crushed foot eventually reached his brain; and wailed even louder when he discovered the loss of his armoury. The dragon wasted no time in seizing on this golden opportunity to add to Bolg's misery, as soon as the last of the troll's missiles had found its target and his pathetic bawling had risen from the general uproar of the crowd, Snarlgard lunged forward to strike at the troll.

His mission accomplished, Jonquil decided that the best way to advance to the tree was to remain in his current prone position and crawl through the moving forest of legs. Suddenly there was a sickening crunch from above and the banf looked up just in time to see Bolg's head being twisted to a most unnatural angle by the gripping jaws of the Autumn dragon. He looked away before the blood-chilling, wrenching sound came to its loud conclusion and began to wriggle his way forward. Then disaster struck, one of the Ice Troll's massive feet trod on Jonquil's left hand, as the monster staggered from side to side under the force of the dragon, pressing it hard into the soggy ground anchoring him like a rock. Try as he might Jonquil could not free himself from the dead monster, who was now only being kept upright by the pressure of the squeezing bodies around him. The roots of the Green Oak were tantalisingly close; but they might just as well have been on the other side of the forest, the banf was stuck fast. The safe end of a clumsily carried spear prodded hard into the base of Jonquil's neck, working its way under the back of his goblin helmet; before the banf had time to act, his head-gear was prised off with such force that it skidded through the mud in front of him, far out of reach. Unfortunately for Jonquil the spear-carrying goblin soldier quickly spotted the banf's distinctly ungoblin-like features and a cry of rage and discovery burst from the hawk-eyed creature's lips. Jonquil tugged and heaved at his trapped hand as the goblin wrestled with his spear to try and turn it around in the heavily cramped conditions. He almost took one of his brethren's eyes out endeavouring to manoeuvre the sharp blade downwards; and very nearly got a sabre in his gut for his trouble.

The mud sucking at Jonquil's hand allowed it to move a little beneath the dead troll's foot, lubricating the front and back of his palm as it eased forward.

The frustrated goblin was almost beside himself with temper, he was furiously attempting to remove the end of his spear from the ornate visor of one of his fellows, the other goblin was pushing frantically at the entangled spear, which now involved at least three other goblins as well. Suddenly the weapon wrenched free of the metal cage with such force that it flew out of control jamming its point into the visor of another goblin standing on the other side, the spear-bearer screeched with fury.

Jonquil was winning, slowly but surely his hand was oozing free, then eventually it 'shlouped!' out and he was thrown backwards with the effort. The banf heaved himself back on to his knees and began to scramble forward.

The goblin was already looking for the banf having snatched his spear clear of obstructions, his eyes focused on Jonquil's exposed back as he scrambled away.

With the evil glint of a frustrated hunter finally about to vanquish his prey, the goblin spear-bearer drew back his arm to thrust. The banf realised the danger just in time and pulled himself into a tight ball on the ground, the goblin's spear nicked the skin on his thigh as it plunged into the mud; but the murderous creature was not giving up yet, as quickly as the weapon had lunged to earth, the goblin drew it back for another strike. Jonquil was helpless, he had saved himself from one fatal thrust only to condemn himself to another; he screwed up his eyes and clenched his teeth to meet the pain; then he thought of Rattajack and all went quiet.

On Thin Ice

The grand procession of the three great dragons started out from the scarred, blackened battle ground. The Sacred Vessels mounted high on their backs. Snarlgard was far too damaged to even hope of flight, so the Guardians had decided that they would all walk to the sea.

By the power of the Fire Orbs, the Wizards of Light had spoken to Rattajack. They told him of their flight to the Forgotten Island and that he must lead the three dragons through the forest following the meandering Green Sky rivers until they married with each other into the festering Poison Swamps and finally the Southern Ocean. Rattajack had answered them in his poignant silent tongue and assured the Lords of the Three Seasons that he would do as they bid him and lead the dragons forward.

Snarlgard had been saved by the eventual arrival of Arangast, who had encountered numerous pockets of resistance along his path to the battle ground. By the time he made his glorious appearance at the Green Oak, his jaws were already dripping with the blood of a hundred enemy creatures. When his eyes had fallen on the terrible sight of the stricken Guardian of Autumn, crawling in stabbing, tearing creatures, the mighty roar of revenge that he had carried with him for so long, burst from the depths of his soul, summoning forth an ocean of white flame that flooded the beaten dragon and the swarms of his attackers.

Most of the evil servants were claimed by the fire and fell in mass smouldering heaps, the rest fled into the forest, some of them hopping and dancing to put out their burning clothes or hair. A few moments after Arangast had entered the Great Battle of the Green Oak, it was over and those goblins, demons and trolls that were still alive were gone.

The Summer dragon had then communicated with Rattajack, Gorgoyle was instructed to send up a high beacon of flame to guide Arangast back to them; and then carrying the Sacred Vessels of Spring and Summer (and the terragon), the two great dragons returned to the Green Oak to tend to their brother.

Snarlgard had been completely unharmed by Arangast's flame as he and his fellow Guardians were impervious to the effects of fire. His injuries looked grievous but the iron thick scales of his hide had saved his body from the worst of the enemy's fury. The most serious damage had been inflicted on his wings, rendering him flightless; and it would take many restful days and skilful healing to make them whole again. There was only one place in the world now where such attention could be solicited, the Forgotten Island of the Wizards.

It took the procession of the dragons many hard days travelling to reach the shores of the river delta, Rattajack was able to uncover occasional outcrops of fungi for sustenance, at various points along the journey.

Arangast had been worried about their having to cross the Poison Swamps that lay at the southernmost fringe of the forest; but when they arrived at the infamous place, they found that for once the freezing grip of Winter had worked in their favour. The whole area of venomous pools had been turned into a lake of ice; the fatal fumes safely sealed beneath a frozen lid for the duration of the dark season. The procession was able to cross the glacial covering without fear and just beyond the Poison Swamps, was the river delta and the sea.

Where once the putrid waters from the swamps had trickled into the cleansing embrace of the ocean waves, there was now a sorcery-wrought landscape of ice. The rolling breakers had been stilled and in their place were rippled sculptures of frozen water. Far out to sea, twin headlands converged to form an almost completely isolated circle of water. The Bay of Voices. The bay was a desert of drifted snow and ice, beyond it a deep blue line edged the horizon, fine dashes of white breaking against the advancing frozen cap.

'He has frozen the sea!' Gorgoyle cried in dismay.

'Only the quieter waters of the bay have been claimed,' Arangast replied, 'The ocean is still free. Look! The waves break in the distance!'

'Perhaps it would be better for us if the ocean had frozen,' Snarlgard sighed, 'then we could walk all the way to the island.'

Arangast turned to the red dragon, 'Better for us perhaps; but disastrous for our masters. The flowing waters that surround the island are their only hope of survival. For as you know, Snarlgard, the foul servants of the Ice Sorcerer cannot bear the pure touch of salt water, it burns their skin. Only when the seas are completely frozen will Vrorst's minions be able to reach the island.'

'Then how do we cross the sea, Arangast?' Gorgoyle asked, 'surely we cannot swim there, with the weight of the Sacred Vessels on our backs?'

'No,' Arangast agreed, 'there has to be another way. We must think of another way!'

'There is another way!' a voice announced, 'we must build a raft!'

'A raft?' Arangast questioned.

'Large enough to carry Snarlgard, Rattajack, the three chests and myself. You, Arangast, and Gorgoyle will provide the propulsion, by flying ahead on long tethers. I've been sitting here thinking the whole thing out, it's simple!' the voice assured.

'Simple, eh?' Arangast said, as he turned to look at the two legs hanging over the edge of the Sacred Vessel of Summer. 'Perhaps you would care to climb down from your lofty perch, Sir, and give us the benefit of your clearly expert knowledge.' Arangast continued.

'Certainly, my dear Arangast,' the voice replied.

The two legs climbed back inside the chest and a face appeared. Jonquil's skin and clothes were black, partly from the quagmire he had been lying in close to the Green Oak and also because of the terrible fire Arangast had breathed over the creatures above him. He would surely have perished in the fierce blaze that killed the spear-bearing goblin just as it was about to deliver its second death-dealing blow, had it not been for the wall of heavily armoured bodies that collapsed on top of him, effectively shielding him from the worst of the fire. The most serious injury he had had to endure was a mildly blistered hand, which had since been thoroughly licked by the terragon and carefully bandaged.

However, the greatest danger to befall the banf had not come from the spears of the enemy, or the volcanic breath of the Summer dragon. The most serious threat to his survival had come when he had lain unconscious beneath the pile of charred enemy creatures and the time came for the Guardians to continue their journey. Arangast had despaired of ever seeing the banf alive again when it became clear that he was not waiting patiently for the end of the battle in the beams of the Green Oak as he had been instructed. The dragons could only assume that Jonquil had either fallen to his death or been taken and killed by the enemy. If it had not been for the stubborn refusal of the terragon to abandon his lifelong friend and the strange dream that had plagued Rattajack's sleep during that night, where the banf seemed to be calling him from a dark, enclosed place, Jonquil would never have been found.

Acting on a vague suggestion from Snarlgard, Rattajack had started sniffing around the roots of the Green Oak, in case his dream had signified that Jonquil had crawled inside them to shelter from the conflict. Within a short while despite the strong smells of burning flesh; and goblin flesh at that, Rattajack picked up the faintest strains of his companion's beloved scent. The great dragons cleared the bodies from around him and Jonquil was recovered.

He had looked quite dead but the terragon knew otherwise and Arangast decreed that Jonquil's unconscious form be laid gently inside the Summer Vessel to be carried to the sea; and after Rattajack had managed a crude imitation of the banf's treevine tying prowess, to secure the three Vessels, the dragons' procession had commenced.

Jonquil climbed down from Arangast's back and led the three dragons back into the forest a short way. He pointed out which trees he considered would make the best raft and then he and Rattajack left the beasts to do the felling whilst they gathered sufficient lengths of treevine to bind the trunks together. As the banf and the terragon watched the dragons at work, they realised just how grateful they were that the Guardians and themselves were on the same side, the dragons were tearing the trunks off their roots with only their bare teeth. By the time the two companions had returned from their collecting, an ample array of roughly severed tree-trunks lay waiting for Jonquil's skills.

Orolan sat alone on his high tower, in the ancient castle of the Brotherhood on the Forgotten Island. He wore a worried expression as he stared into the gently glowing depths of the Summer Fire Orb. Strange pictures had flashed before his eyes; immense armies of Winter, gathering against the light of the Sacred Vessels, a Guardian in distress, a great searching fire, a frozen bay; The Bay of Voices.

Now the crystal sphere was vague, the pictures floating within it were blurred and shapeless, their meaning obscured. Perhaps this too was the work of the Ice Sorcerer, his power reaching out across the sea to blind them. Orolan had called before him three fairies of the seasons; Mimmer of Spring, Cellandia of Summer and Fossfex of Autumn.

These three delicate spirits were to seek for the Mer-folk, that dwelled within the paradise gardens beneath the sea. The Bay of Voices was the place where legend decreed the Mer-folk came ashore to sing their songs of joy and love, for the light of the world and all things noble and free. Orolan's message was for them to go there now, to help save the very source of the light of the world that they claimed to love so well. The fairies departed and the Summer Wizard lowered his tired head until his brow rested against the cool skin of the Fire Orb; and then he prayed.

The hefty, substantial raft slid out over the frozen water, the three chests of power had been securely lashed to the logs and two thickly plaited reins had been tied to the bows of the crude vessel. The dragons and the two companions moved out over the ice towards the middle of the frozen bay.

Suddenly a distant ugly voice cried out and the wall of trees that surrounded the bay began to move. Dark figures rapidly moved out from beneath the shadowy trees, a vast crescent of Winter warriors swiftly closing in on the raft. Arangast saw that they would never make it to the open sea before the enemy sealed the gap. Battalions of goblins and trolls trotted out across the ice towards them, chanting marching songs as they approached; Legions of Icedemons, carrying the standards of the Ice Sorcerer stamped across the frozen water, some carrying drums to beat their steps. Even at the distance the demons were from the raft, the dragons and the companions could see them gnashing their teeth and spitting obscenities in their direction. There were great Snowdragons stalking through the hordes, black witches rode their backs in silver saddles, the white beasts flapped their wings with impatience, eager to swoop into the fray. The noble creatures had been caught in the enemy's trap, out in the open with their raft, which suddenly seemed so useless, to witness before they died, the awesome array of the Ice Sorcerer's armoury which closed on them in an ever decreasing circle, the greatest force of soldiers and beasts he had ever compiled up to yet; and they carried torches, torches with which to burn the Sacred Vessels.

Jonquil looked fearfully at Rattajack and this time there was no comfort in those dazzling orbs, only the reflection of the approaching armies and the cold light of doom.

The tightening noose of Winter monsters was given the order to halt; and Prince Bledderag stepped to the fore, one of the few survivors from the Battle of the Green Oak. His expression was one of hate in its purest form and his eyes glowed with his lust for murder. He held the twin battle clubs aloft, that had now become his symbol; and his mouth fell open to deliver the word of attack.

Suddenly a volley of racing, pale-grey shapes swept underneath the ice in twisting circles and spirals. No-one other than Jonquil and Rattajack seemed to notice them, there were hundreds; weaving beneath the waiting columns of Winter creatures in great clustered schools, darting back and forth beneath the raft. Jonquil thought he could make out heads and arms and perhaps long,

Orolan, Lord of Summer, strange pictures had flashed before his eyes!

flowing hair on some of the fast-swimming shadows but they had the tails of fishes, that much was quite clear.

Suddenly an ear-splitting sound burst into his head, a single, screeching voice grating violently on his senses, then the cry was taken up by every single creature in the surrounding armies . . .

'. . . D E S T R O Y ! ! '

The adventure continues . . .

The Wizards' Realms of Enchantica